Alfred Hitchcock's
Ghostly Gallery

"This is a book of ghost stories," says Alfred Hitchcock in his introduction, "and is designed both to frighten and instruct."

Mr. Hitchcock has selected stories by nine famous ghost writers to prove his point. To see if he succeeds, read on!

Alfred Hitchcock's
Ghostly Gallery

Illustrated by Fred Banbery

Random House   New York

This title was originally cataloged by the Library of Congress as follows:
Hitchcock, Alfred Joseph, 1899–   ed.
Ghostly gallery; [eleven spooky stories for young people]   Illustrated by Fred Banbery.   New York, Random House [1962]   206 p.   illus.   26 cm.
1. Detective and mystery stories.   2. Children's stories.   I. Title.
PZ5.H64Gh   62–14298 ‡
ISBN: 0-394-81226-3   ISBN: 0-394-91226-8 (lib. ed.)

The editor gratefully acknowledges the invaluable assistance of Robert Arthur in the preparation of this volume and thanks the following for permission to include copyrighted material: A. P. Watt & Son and the executors of the Estate of the late H. G. Wells for "The Truth About Pyecraft," from *Short Stories of H. G. Wells;* Brandt & Brandt for "Miss Emmeline Takes Off" by Walter R. Brooks, first published in *The Saturday Evening Post,* Copyright, 1945, by The Curtis Publishing Company; Robert Arthur for "The Haunted Trailer," Copyright, 1941, by *Weird Tales* under the original title of "Death Thumbs A Ride," Robert Arthur and Popular Publications, Inc. for "The Wonderful Day," Copyright, 1940, as "Miracle on Main Street" by Popular Publications, Inc. and "Obstinate Uncle Otis," Copyright, 1941, by Popular Publications; Harold Matson Company for "Housing Problem" by Henry Kuttner, Copyright, 1944, by Street and Smith and reprinted from *Charm Magazine;* Arkham House for "In A Dim Room" from *The Fourth Book of Jorkens,* Copyright, 1948, by Lord Dunsany; Stephen Aske, literary agent, for "The Waxwork" by A. M. Burrage, © Stephen Aske, London; Willis Kingsley Wing and The Public Trustee, Administrator of the Estate of the late Algernon Blackwood, for "The Valley of the Beasts" from *The Wolves of God and Other Fey Stories,* Copyright, 1921, by E. P. Dutton & Co., Inc., renewed 1949 by Algernon Blackwood.

iv

Introduction

Good evening, and welcome to Alfred Hitchcock's Ghostly Gallery. This is your perennial host speaking. It seems to me that I am continually introducing things. Through my motion pictures, I introduce new stars; in television, I introduce the commercials, and now—here I am again. In this instance, I presume, you would call me a ghost host.

I don't want to appear disloyal to television, but I think reading will be good for you. After all, your television tube may burn out some day. Furthermore, you need practice for reading the subtitles in those foreign movies. But don't be discouraged. You'll get used to reading. Turning all these pages may be difficult, but the exercise will do you good.

While we were preparing this book there was one mad moment when someone suggested that we add a sound track. This is fine for furnishing laughter for comedy television shows, but assorted screams, wails, moans and clanking chains aren't good in book form. Oh, the problem was solved *technically,* but there was still one drawback. Public librarians became quite overwrought because people were opening the books in the reading rooms and the din was tremendous. As a result you will read these stories as they were meant to be read—in stereophonic silence.

But now I should say a word about the type of story you will find lurking between these covers. After all, I don't want you to begin this book under false pretenses. This is not *David Copperfield* or *Rebecca of Sunnybrook Farm.* This is a book of ghost stories and is designed both to frighten and instruct. You see, my aim is to teach you about ghosts and I feel you will be a very sympathetic audience. Let me explain.

The two most misunderstood groups in our society are teenagers and ghosts. When an adult hears a screech (of tires?) sounding through the night air, who gets the blame? When hub caps mysteriously disappear, whose fault is it? I am sure you are already feeling more sympathetic toward our ectoplasmic friends.

A ghost's life is not as happy and carefree as you would think. They must live in dark, damp places. They are usually denied human companionship. How often have you deliberately avoided some secluded spot simply because you knew a ghost was haunting the place? For shame! Think how lonely he must have been.—And this is precisely why they are mischievous. They are simply trying to attract attention. I'm sure you have done the same thing.—When you were much younger, of course.

My message is simply this: Be kind to ghosts. And whatever you do, don't scream when you see one. People are always doing this to the poor souls and turning them into nervous wrecks.

But now it is time for you to browse through my gallery. This is not a one-man show. The gallery is featuring nine of the very best ghost writers. Pick out a story and read it. That will make you one-tenth of a ghost. Then proceed with the others. I know you will enjoy yourselves, and the next time you see my friendly apparition rising from inside your television tube, I trust you will feel a new friendship toward a fellow spirit.

—*Alfred Hitchcock*

Contents

Alfred Hitchcock's

Ghostly Gallery

Miss Emmeline Takes Off

Walter Brooks

When the old Valiant house on the lake was sold for taxes, Miss Emmeline Valiant went to live at Mrs. Purdy's. She took very little with her. She took Thomas, her cat, and her family portraits. The rest of the things were sold to Mr. Maule, who had bought the house.

Mr. Maule offered her a lump sum for everything. It was not a generous offer, although it was made with many protestations of sympathy and respect and with a sort of codicil in which Mr. Maule said that he was sorry he was not a rich man so that he could offer her more. Miss Emmeline replied that she did not see that his financial standing had any relation to the value of the goods, and that, in any case, neither emotional nor financial hypocrisy was necessary, since all she wanted was to get it over with. If he would give her a check the matter was closed. So he wrote the check.

Afterward he did a lot of grumbling about ingratitude and stiff-necked pride, but nobody paid much attention. For everybody in the village knew that Miss Emmeline had several times in the past offered him the house at a fair price, and each time he had refused, preferring to buy it in cheap at a forced sale. And indeed it was suspected that it was his influence that had forced the sale.

Of course, nobody dared say this to Mr. Maule. Although he had retired from active business, he was rich and influential. He had given the village a park, and it was known that he intended to do a lot of entertaining, which is good for local trade and also for people who like to go to parties. Also, the old Valiant house itself was so enveloped in tradition that it was felt whoever occupied it was by that fact alone entitled to respect.

So when this story begins it is evening and Mr. Maule is sitting in the Valiant house gloating, and Miss Emmeline is sitting in her room at Mrs. Purdy's stroking Thomas, her cat, and wondering what she will live on when Mr. Maule's check is used up. The Valiants were one of those families of early settlers who colonized the country by moving slowly westward from the Eastern seaboard.

The movement was not even. The colonists progressed like grasshoppers, in a series of hops. Sometimes they would hop several times in a generation and sometimes there would be a century between hops. The Valiants had been hundred-year hoppers. They came over in sixteen-something to Massachusetts and then in seventeen-something they had hopped to Connecticut, and in 1810 they had hopped into New York State. One granduncle had hopped on into Ohio and disappeared, but the rest of the family had stayed put and had lived and died in the old house on the lake. All but Miss Emmeline, who now sat pondering past glories and future doubts.

All at once Miss Emmeline jumped up and said, "Oh!" For she had suddenly remembered that, in the confusion and unhappiness of leaving the home where she had lived all her life, she had forgotten to bring with her something more precious to her than the portraits or even Thomas, her cat. She had forgotten the queer little flat trunk which was said to have belonged to an ancestress who had figured in one of the New England witch trials.

Now, in the scale of New England genealogical values, a witch is equivalent to a patent of nobility. A judge is better than a minister, and a governor is better than a judge, but an ancestress who was actually hanged for witchcraft is a rare and glittering treasure. So Miss Emmeline took a clean handkerchief and put on her hat and went to see Mr. Maule.

Her visit delighted Mr. Maule, for he felt that it would give him an opportunity to try out the formal Old World courtesy which he conceived to be appropriate in his new setting. But Miss Emmeline cut through his polished ineptitudes to come straight to the point. She had forgotten the trunk. Would he permit her to send for it?

Now, I suppose Mr. Maule didn't particularly want the trunk, but the discovery that Miss Emmeline's call was not a social one, after all, made him resentful, and he said no. The trunk, he said, was part of the house furnishings for which he had paid. After all, he said, a bargain was a bargain.

"Then will you permit me to purchase it back from you?" Miss Emmeline said.

Again he said no, and while he was defending this position Miss Emmeline bowed stiffly and walked out of the house.

Well, Miss Emmeline was pretty upset. It had upset her to go into her own house again and see all the familiar things around her and realize that she had no legal right there. It upset her to feel more strongly than ever that Mr. Maule was not the sort of person she wanted to have using those things. And it upset her completely to realize that she had so carelessly let the most treasured of her heirlooms pass out of her hands.

But not quite completely. That evening she sat looking out of the window of her room at Mrs. Purdy's. She had selected that room because from it she could see the lake and the old Valiant house standing solid and firm among its gardens on the little bluff overlooking the water. She sat with Thomas, her cat, on her knees and looked out, and she could not see much because the moon would not be up until later. But she could see the lights in the Valiant house, and when the last one winked out she waited another half hour, and then she put her hat on and went quietly down the stairs.

She met no one on the street. She went in through the side gate and across the lawn to the back door. It would be locked, but she knew that lock. If you jiggled it gently, the latch would spring. She had never had it repaired because it was handy if she happened to lock herself out. With her shoes in her hand, she went quietly through the dining room and hall and up the stairs and past a door behind which some very vulgar snoring was going on, and up the attic stairs.

It was lighter in the attic, for a lopsided moon had risen above the hills across the lake. The solid old floor did not creak once as she crept across it and carefully opened the back window under which stood the trunk. It was very small —about as large as a medium-sized suitcase—and would be easy to carry down the stairs. But she felt it would be safer to lower it from the window by the clothesline which was coiled near by.

But there was one thing more she needed. The attic had not been cleaned since last fall. If her footprints were not to be found in the dust on the floor, she must drag something over them before she left. From a far corner she brought a broom—an old handmade affair with a bundle of twigs bound to the end of a short stick—which probably antedated the house.

But when she lifted the trunk to slide it over the window sill, something rattled inside. She had thought it empty— though indeed she never remembered having opened it. It had always been just "the trunk"—so precious that it had never been shown to anyone outside the family, but always kept in that one place underneath the attic window. She had oiled it once a year to preserve the leather, but she had oiled only the outside.

The hasp was stiff, but she got it open. The thing that had rattled was a flat metal box, and she was able to make out that it contained some sort of ointment with a bitter but not unpleasant medicated smell. She tucked it into her jacket pocket, but when she closed the trunk again she scratched her wrist deeply on the hasp. The scratch bled a little, and, without thinking much about it, she took out the box again and smeared some of the ointment on the place and rubbed it in. For she had been brought up in a school which always treated small cuts and abrasions with a liberal coating of any salve that happened to be handy.

But as she was putting the box back into her pocket, it slipped out of her hand and clattered on the floor boards. She snatched it up quickly, then stood listening. She knew that Mr. Maule's servants must be occupying the rooms directly beneath her. For a minute she thought they hadn't heard anything. Then there were vague sounds downstairs, and a voice called. Miss Emmeline knew she was trapped. She seized the broom with an instinctive impulse to defend the stairs, but, before she had realized how foolish that was, something else happened.

The tingling she had noticed in her wrist when she had first applied the ointment suddenly shot up her arm and spread to her whole body. She felt curiously lightheaded, and wondered if she was going to faint. The broom on which she was trying to lean behaved in a most unaccountable manner, for it leaped in her hands and seemed to be pulling her toward the window. And then, as she grasped it more tightly, she felt her feet leave the floor; they scraped over the window sill and she was moving rapidly through the air twenty feet above the garden. But the broomstick was still firmly clasped in her hands, and she realized that she was flying swiftly eastward into the rising moon.

Dear me, this is very odd, thought Miss Emmeline. And indeed the experience was unusual, and would have been very disturbing to her if she had had time to think about it. But, of course, she didn't. What was most immediately puzzling was how she managed to keep from falling off. She was riding sidesaddle, which was, in a way, reassuring, but there was no sense of weight or of sitting on anything. The buoyancy was in herself, and the broomstick, as she presently discovered, was only for steering; though, if left to itself, it guided her due east. *Just like old Captain,* she thought, *when I gave him his head and he made for home.*

Then a disquieting idea wedged itself into her thoughts: *Where would home be for a broomstick?* Miss Emmeline was no fool, and she realized that she had stumbled on the professional secrets of that ancestress who had—and quite properly—been hanged as a witch. The ointment was certainly that famous salve with which the witches anointed themselves before taking off for the Sabbath. Then was the broomstick headed for the Sabbath? Although it was a good old New England custom, Miss Emmeline did not feel quite up to the rather robust form of entertainment which she understood was there provided. She pulled the broomstick around and headed northward up the lake.

She skimmed low over the dark water, then rose higher and circled back over the village. *Dear me,* she thought, *this is quite exhilarating.* But it was late and the air was getting chilly. *And, after all,* she thought, *this flying around is most enjoyable, but the important thing is the trunk, and I still haven't got it. I must think out another plan.* She flew up Main Street and circled the Presbyterian Church steeple three times; then, assuring herself that no one was in sight, swooped down and alighted in Mrs. Purdy's side yard. With the broom under her arm, she let herself quietly in and went up to her room. It wasn't until she had finally got into bed that she remembered she had left her shoes in the attic.

Well, Miss Emmeline spent all the next morning in the public library, reading up about witches. As far as she could make out, they had been an extraordinarily ineffectual lot. They had claimed to be able to dry up cows and raise storms and give children fits. But, even when they confessed, it seemed difficult to prove that they got results. They also made little wax figures of their enemies and stuck pins in the parts of the body which they wished to afflict. Miss Emmeline was unable to find, in the few references available, any account of the procedure and, in any case, could not see what use she could make of such accomplishments. For Mr. Maule had neither cows nor children, and if she raised a storm he would just close the windows. *And, anyway,* she thought, *I don't want to harm him. I just want my trunk. And my shoes,* she added. For, indeed, the loss of a pair of shoes was a serious matter.

Well, Miss Emmeline thought and thought, but she could not think of a plan, and she decided that, although being a witch was entertaining, it had little practical value.

On her way home from the library, she met her old friend, Mrs. Courtney Bishop. Mrs. Bishop was brusque and autocratic, but not with Miss Emmeline, of whom she was very fond. They had gone to school together as girls and their friendship had, rather amazingly, survived a widening divergence in fortune, for the Bishops had gone up as fast as the Valiants had gone down. Perhaps because, although Mrs. Bishop had often offered to help Miss Emmeline, the latter had always refused.

Miss Emmeline learned from Mrs. Bishop that there had been a disturbance at Mr. Maule's the previous night. There had been noises in the attic, and the shoes and the open window had been found, but no explanation seemed possible, as there had been no one there and the window was twenty feet from the ground. Mr. Maule pooh-poohed the whole thing, but the servants were frightened and, as one might have expected, the cook asserted that she had seen a great black creature fly away from the window across the lake.

Miss Emmeline did not smile, but her mouth twitched slightly, and Mrs. Bishop looked at her sharply and said, "You know something about this, Emmeline."

Miss Emmeline, who always told the exact truth, said, "Yes, I do." She frowned and, after a moment's hesitation, said, "I think I had better tell you about it."

"Well, you had better come to dinner tonight," said Mrs. Bishop. "But if you are going to the Girls' Friendly meeting, we must get along or we will be late."

"Oh, yes, the Girls' Friendly," said Miss Emmeline. "I had forgotten."

"Forgotten the Girls' Friendly?" said Mrs. Bishop, raising her eyebrows.

And Miss Emmeline said, "Yes, and I—I think I had better not go."

Mrs. Bishop raised her eyebrows another notch, but all she said was "Well, dinner at seven," and went on.

During dinner, nothing was said about Mr. Maule, but afterward, when coffee had been cleared away and they were alone in the big living room, which looked out through huge windows eastward across the lake and north across the Valiant garden, Miss Emmeline told just what had happened. As the story went on, Mrs. Bishop's eyes opened wider and wider, and then her mouth opened and she sat forward in her chair. But when Miss Emmeline came to the part about flying out of the window on the broom, she brought her hand down hard on the chair arm and said, "Stop!" So Miss Emmeline stopped.

"Where are you going?" Mrs. Bishop demanded, as Miss Emmeline got up.

"Just to the hall to get something I brought with me," Miss Emmeline said, "for I knew you would think I had lost my mind." And in a minute she came back with something wrapped up in a dark table cover, and undid it, and it was her broom.

"Oh, yes, we have one of those things," said Mrs. Bishop, "and I suppose you—ah—flew about on it?"

"You can humor me if it amuses you, Letty," said Miss Emmeline, "but please don't edge toward the door, for I assure you I am quite harmless. And if my demonstration fails I will call Doctor Blessing myself and ask him to come over. This is the ointment," she said, holding it out, and Mrs. Bishop sniffed and said, "Pew!"

So Miss Emmeline rolled up the screen that covered the open window, rubbed some ointment on her wrist, and took her broom in both hands. Then, with a slow and quite dignified motion, she rose from the floor and sailed out the window. Mrs. Bishop fainted away.

After a few minutes, Mrs. Bishop came to. She moaned a little, but nobody answered, so she sat up and looked around and then she hurried to the window. It was pretty dark, but a lot of the Valiant windows were lit, and in the reflected light she saw something big and black swoop past the corner of the porch. Then, in a minute, it came back just a few feet above the lawn, and she saw that it was Miss Emmeline, who waved her handkerchief as she passed. Mrs. Bishop thought she would faint away again. Then she decided that a glass of lemonade would be better. She got it herself from the dining room, and while she was sipping it, Miss Emmeline flew in the window and leaned her broom in the corner and sat down again. "Well," she said, "now do you believe me?"

"No," said Mrs. Bishop, "and I suppose it is some form of hypnotism, and I will ask you not to do it again."

"Suppose you try it yourself then," said Miss Emmeline, and held out the ointment. Mrs. Bishop said she would do nothing of the kind, but Miss Emmeline argued that if she didn't believe it, it would do no harm to try. She said, "If it doesn't work with you, I will believe that there is some hypnotic trickery about it, and I will promise you not to do it again."

So Mrs. Bishop at last agreed. And, although she was rather stout, she rose from the floor as lightly as a feather and floated out of the window.

After about ten minutes, there was a scream, and then a great clamor and shouting over in the Valiant garden, but as Miss Emmeline started up in alarm Mrs. Bishop came through the window. She seemed a little flushed, and as she sat down she said, "Well, Emmeline, you have proved your point, and I must say it is very delightful, but it won't do. It won't do at all."

So Miss Emmeline asked what had happened, and Mrs. Bishop said that, coming back, she had had some trouble with the steering apparatus. She had not realized that if you depressed the stick, you swooped toward the ground. Unfortunately, she had swooped just at the wrong moment and had passed so close between Mr. Maule and the maid who was serving him coffee on the terrace that she had scared them both into fits.

"But I don't think they recognized me," she said.

"It doesn't matter if they did," Miss Emmeline said, "for they wouldn't believe their own eyes."

"That is all very well," said Mrs. Bishop, "but sooner or later someone will see you, Emmeline, and while you are certainly old enough at seventy to do as you please, still, flying around the country on a broomstick is going to cause talk. I'm sure I don't know what your dear father would have said."

"I don't either," said Miss Emmeline, "and I don't care. I had rather hoped," she said, "that you and I might find it a pleasant diversion for these warm summer evenings, Letty. It is so much pleasanter if there is someone to talk to. However, if you feel that way about it—"

"You have no one, Emmeline," said Mrs. Bishop, "but I have my grandchildren to consider. And there is another point: You may say you have done nothing wrong, but I am not so sure, and if you could only speak to the rector—"

Miss Emmeline said that Mr. Cook was very modern, and wouldn't believe a word of it. And she said, "If the devil can quote Scripture for his purpose, why can't a good churchgoer use the devil's methods for hers?"

Well, oddly enough, this argument convinced Mrs. Bishop. She was glad to be convinced anyway, for now that she had recovered from the excitement of such an incredible experience she remembered how delightful it had been, and particularly how the twinges of rheumatism, which bothered her almost continually nowadays, had not twinged once. And the long and the short of it was that Miss Emmeline didn't have much trouble persuading her to try it again. So she went and got a broom and assured herself that the servants were busy in the back of the house, and then she and Miss Emmeline went for what she later referred to as a delightful little spin around the lake.

In the meantime, Mr. Maule, after recovering from his fright, was profoundly disturbed. He had not recognized Mrs. Bishop, but both he and the maid were prepared to swear that it was an old lady on a broomstick who had swooped upon them and who, after rising again, had seemed to fly into the Bishop window. So, after the housekeeper had got the maid quieted down, and put to bed, he decided to go over and investigate. He told the maid who answered the bell that he had seen someone climb in the living-room window.

"Mrs. Bishop and Miss Valiant are there, I think," said the maid, and led him to the living-room door. But when she opened it the room was empty.

"Miss Valiant, eh?" said Mr. Maule thoughtfully. "Well,

perhaps they'll be back, and I'd better wait and warn them."

So the maid said, "All right," and left. And Mr. Maule was just sitting down when Miss Emmeline and Mrs. Bishop sailed through the window. Mr. Maule gave a whoop and made it back to his own front door in eight seconds flat.

Well, I guess Mr. Maule had scared the two old ladies as much as they had scared him, almost. And after they had each had a large glass of lemonade, Mrs. Bishop said, "Well, Emmeline, this has all been a great mistake, and if you will take my advice you will throw that ointment into the lake." She was pretty cross, so Miss Emmeline put the ointment in her pocket and wrapped up her broom and went home.

Well, nothing happened for a day or two, and then one afternoon young Mr. John Sawyer came to see Miss Emmeline.

"Why, it is very nice of you to come see me, John," Miss Emmeline said. "And how is your dear mother?" Mr. Sawyer said his mother was all right, and he looked at Miss Emmeline so oddly that she said, "Why, what is the matter? Don't you feel well?"

"Well, I feel rather foolish," said Mr. Sawyer, "for Mr. Maule has been to see me and—Well, I thought I ought to see you about it. I wouldn't have come," he said, "but, as you know, I have handled Mr. Maule's business here locally and I had no choice. He—really it is too foolish for words—he charges you with witchcraft."

"Dear me," said Miss Emmeline, "but is witchcraft a crime?"

"Heavens, I don't know!" said Mr. Sawyer. "But what he specifically wants is to get a court order restraining you from flying over his property."

Miss Emmeline smiled and said, "Is the man really serious about this?"

Mr. Sawyer said, "He seems to be, but what I really think he wants is to make you look ridiculous in the eyes of the village and, of course, I think he could get the order at the county seat, because he has Judge Simmons in his pocket." Mr. Sawyer got up. "No, really, Miss Emmeline," he said. "I just thought I ought to tell you. I intend to give up Mr. Maule's business, for the man is certainly cracked. He had the most idiotic story about you and Mrs. Bishop. But I can't think of anything that we can do to stop him."

"You certainly mustn't give up his business, John," said Miss Emmeline. "There aren't too many wealthy clients in this village. And I think you should advise him not to get that order, for he doesn't understand this village very well if he thinks it would make me look ridiculous. It would merely make him appear a very boorish practical joker. And for my part, I will promise not to fly over his property on my broomstick any more."

Mr. Sawyer laughed heartily at the idea of Miss Emmeline flying around on a broomstick, and the quite truthful details she gave him about the practices of witchcraft he found very entertaining. He asked her if she could raise tempests, and she said she had never tried, but the technique was quite simple.

"Well," he said, "you might try next week when Mr. Maule has his housewarming. I understand it will be a big garden party if the weather is good. And indeed he has gone so wholly early American since buying your house that if you arrived on a broomstick he would be delighted." And when Mr. Sawyer got up to go, he said, "Now be careful about this flying around, Miss Emmeline. Because even if Mr. Maule can't hold you on a witchcraft charge, he can always get you grounded for flying without a license."

Evidently, Mr. Maule took Mr. Sawyer's advice, for Miss Emmeline heard no more about the order. Two days later, Mrs. Bishop called up and asked her to dinner. Miss Emmeline smiled, because she knew Mrs. Bishop pretty well, and she said to Thomas, her cat, "Well, well, Thomas, what did

I tell you? And I guess I had better take my broom along."
So she did, and it was just as she had thought. After a good
deal of beating about the bush, Mrs. Bishop brought up the
flying business, and at last said that, although such goings-on
were both undignified and reprehensible, there was no great
harm in their taking one more flight, if it was the last one.

So, as it was a chilly evening, she put on her mink coat
and lent Miss Emmeline a sealskin jacket, and they flew down
to Crandall Hollow and poked around in the old cemetery
with a flashlight, looking for Bishop and Crandall tombstones.
Old Jed Holly saw the light flickering among the graves as
he was weaving homeward, and never drank another drop
again as long as he lived. So they did some good, as well as
having a good time. And before she went home Miss Emmeline put some of her ointment in a little silver box on a
side table and Mrs. Bishop pretended not to see her.

The day of Mr. Maule's housewarming, Miss Emmeline was
fussing around in Mrs. Purdy's garden. She was not so far
from the Valiant house but that she could hear the rattle of
crockery and the roar of polite conversation, and a tide of
resentment rose in her breast, and she remembered what Mr.
Sawyer had said about raising a tempest. So she knelt down
and picked up some dirt and threw it over her shoulder, muttering the cabalistic words she had read in the encyclopedia,
along with the names of several important fiends who had
charge of such matters. She would never have done it if she
had thought she would really get results. She was horrified
when the sunlight swiftly faded from the garden around her
and a sudden gale whipped through the branches, rolling up
great black clouds that swept just above the treetops and
exploded in a series of blinding flashes and terrific thunder
peals, immediately drowned in torrents of driving rain.

Well, it was the father and mother of a storm, and the
garden party was a mess. Nobody had time even to get in-

doors, and all the guests were soaked and, naturally, they blamed Mr. Maule.

So the next day he came to see Miss Emmeline. "You win," he said. "Here's your trunk and your shoes, and now will you lay off me?"

"Thank you," said Miss Emmeline, "and I must tell you that I had no idea the spell would really work, though perhaps I would have done it anyway."

"Well, please don't try any more spells," he said. And then he said, "How do you do it? You can at least explain to me?"

Well, Miss Emmeline looked at Mr. Maule, and she saw a little man who, though, of course, perfectly impossible, was, for all his money and power, unsure and dissatisfied. Things were not all pie for him. For, though he had hired a corps of genealogists and had a fine old house and fine old heirlooms, he shone only with reflected glory. For the house was still the Valiant house, not the Maule house. And she realized that neither of them had what they wanted. She lacked the money to maintain her prestige, and he lacked the position to make his money count. So she felt sorry for him, and asked him to sit down, and then she told him all about it.

Now, if this were a fairy story, we would have Mr. Maule's sympathy aroused, and he would give Miss Emmeline back her house and her things. But the truth is the Mr. Maule felt no sympathy whatever. He was afraid of what Miss Emmeline could do, but if he could buy her good will with the trunk, he wasn't going to offer anything else. And then it occurred to him that the witch ointment would have tremendous commercial possibilities if he could get the formula. He asked a lot of questions about it and offered to buy it. At first Miss Emmeline refused to sell, but that only made him more determined, and when he got up to a price for one quarter of her supply which was more than the house and its contents had cost him, she took it. For she was no fool. And when he said suspiciously, "How do I know this is the real stuff?" she said, "You try it, and if it doesn't work, bring it back and I will return your check."

Well, he tried it all right. Early next morning a farmer named Willett started from home with his milk, and as he came over Five-Mile Hill he saw something big and black struggling feebly in the telegraph wires that run along the railroad track. He got ladders and ropes and took an hour to get Mr. Maule down, and one of Willett's summer boarders took a picture of it and sent it to Squint. It was published as one of the great puzzle pictures of the year, for nobody could explain how Mr. Maule had got up there, least of all Mr. Maule himself. All over the country, people laughed and wondered about it, and in the village they laughed so much that Mr. Maule stayed indoors all the rest of the summer and there were no more parties at the Valiant house. In the fall, when he found that people were still laughing, he closed up the house and offered it for sale.

In the meantime, the chemist to whom Mr. Maule had sent the ointment did succeed in isolating the various ingredients, which were aconite and belladonna and bat's blood and one or two things I shall not tell you about. He had done some reading in the use of drugs in medieval times, and he went to see Mr. Maule in his office in the Empire State Building and told him what he suspected.

"You are quite right," said Mr. Maule, "and I believe we have something which will bring about more profound changes in American life than even the automobile. And the name of Maule will be greater than that of Ford. And you," he said, "shall be managing director of the company, with a salary which, I assure you, will be greater than anything you could make by trying to develop it independently."

"Oh, you can trust me to see that," said the chemist, "but how does it work?"

"Like this," said Mr. Maule. "You rub a little on your wrist—" and he suited the action to the word.

And immediately, with a triumphant smile on his face, he floated out of the window. But as he had no broom to steer with, he rose swiftly in the air and passed out of sight in an easterly direction, and there is really no use speculating where he ended up, for he was never seen again. And the chemist very sensibly tore up his notes and went home and forgot about it.

Well, twice a week all the rest of the summer, Mrs. Bishop invited Miss Emmeline to dinner, and after dinner, if the weather was good, she sent the maids to the movies and the two old ladies flew.

It was the moonlight nights they liked best, when they could watch their shadows glide across the dim fields or, if there were scattered clouds, they could rise through them and look down upon their moonlit contours or plunge through blind dampness to play a dignified game of tag among them.

Now, when Mr. Maule had left the village, he had commissioned Mr. Sawyer to sell the Valiant house and its contents for the best offer he could get. But such old houses are hard to get rid of and, though he had advertised widely, the only offer he had got was from a real-estate man who wanted to buy it cheap for speculation. Mr. Sawyer wrote to Mr. Maule, but got no answer, and, as his instructions were definite, he was about to close the deal when he thought he'd speak to Miss Emmeline first.

"Why, John," said Miss Emmeline, "that is less than Mr. Maule paid me just for the furnishings."

"If you were willing to bid five dollars more," said Mr. Sawyer, "I would have to accept."

So Miss Emmeline wrote him a check and he made out the

papers and gave her the keys, and she moved back in that afternoon.

And Mr. Sawyer sent the check to Mr. Maule's office, and Mr. Maule's secretary deposited it to his personal account, and the money may be there yet, for all I know.

Well, Miss Emmeline was so happy to get back into her old home that she wasn't so much interested in flying for a while, and Mrs. Bishop had to fly by herself.

Mrs. Bishop didn't mind much, because by this time she had become so enthusiastic that she would have flown in broad sunlight if no other time of day had been possible. And indeed she often started out earlier and came home later than she should have, for, in spite of her conventional code, she had always done exactly as she pleased, with little regard to what others might think.

So it came about that first one and then another of the villagers saw her winging homeward at dawn or clear over the lake in the light of the setting sun. Until she was recognized, some alarm was felt and there was a lot of talk, but as soon as people knew who it was the talk died down. For whatever the Bishops did had been approved by the village for several generations, and it now merely felt a quiet pride in this new manifestation of Bishop superiority. And what would have seemed ostentation in a person who was merely very rich, and eccentricity in one who had only social position with little capital to support it, appeared quite right and natural in one who possessed both these titles to consideration.

So now, at the end of the story, we have Miss Emmeline and Thomas, her cat, back in the calm enjoyment of their old home, and Mrs. Bishop—well, to tell you the truth, I do not quite know what to say about Mrs. Bishop. For her flyng, which had been merely a harmless hobby, now seems to have become something more. Curious sounds and ominous presences have been several times reported by her maids, and on several occasions she has disappeared for a week or more at a time. And on the last occasion when the two old ladies took a turn about the lake in the cool of the evening, Miss Emmeline had the disquieting feeling that they were not alone. It may be significant that Mrs. Bishop no longer attends the meetings of the Girls' Friendly Society and that her pew on Sundays is now more often empty than not. But you must draw your own conclusions. I feel, with Miss Emmeline, that the matter is now out of our hands.

The Valley of the Beasts

Algernon Blackwood

As they emerged suddenly from the dense forest the Indian halted, and Grimwood, his employer, stood beside him, gazing into the beautiful wooded valley that lay spread below them in the blaze of a golden sunset. Both men leaned upon their rifles, caught by the enchantment of the unexpected scene.

"We camp here," said Tooshalli abruptly, after a careful survey. "Tomorrow we make a plan."

He spoke excellent English. The note of decision, almost of authority, in his voice was noticeable, but Grimwood set it down to the natural excitement of the moment. Every track they had followed during the last two days, but one track in particular as well, had headed straight for the remote and hidden valley, and the sport promised to be unusual.

"That's so," he replied, in the tone of one giving an order. "You can make camp ready at once." And he sat down on a fallen hemlock tree to take off his moccasin boots and grease feet that ached from the arduous day now drawing to a close.

Though under ordinary circumstances he would have pushed on for another hour or two, he was not averse to a night here. Exhaustion had come upon him during the last bit of rough going, his eye and muscles were no longer steady, and it was doubtful if he could have shot straight enough to kill. He did not mean to miss a second time.

With his Canadian friend Iredale, the latter's half-breed, and his own Indian, Tooshalli, Grimwood had set out three weeks ago to find the "wonderful big moose" the Indians reported were traveling in the Snow River country. They soon found that the tale was true; tracks were abundant; they saw fine animals nearly every day. These carried good heads, but the hunters expected better still and left them alone. Pushing up the river to a chain of small lakes near its source, they then separated into two parties, each with its nine-foot bark canoe, and packed in for three days after the yet bigger animals the Indians agreed would be found in the deeper woods beyond. Excitement was keen, expectation keener still. The day before they separated, Iredale shot the biggest moose of his life, and its head, bigger even than the grand Alaskan heads, hangs in his house today. Grimwood's hunting blood was fairly up. His blood was of the fiery, not to say ferocious, quality. It almost seemed he liked killing for its own sake.

Four days after the party broke into two he came upon a gigantic track, whose measurements and length of stride keyed every nerve he possessed to its highest tension.

Tooshalli examined the tracks for some minutes with care. "It is the biggest moose in the world," he said at length, a new expression on his inscrutable red visage.

Following it all that day, they yet got no sight of the big fellow that seemed to be frequenting a little marshy dip of country where willow and undergrowth abounded. He had not yet scented his pursuers. They were after him again at dawn. Toward the evening of the second day Grimwood caught a sudden glimpse of the monster among a thick clump of willows, and the sight of the magnificent head that easily beat all records set his heart beating like a hammer with excitement. He aimed and fired. But the moose, instead of crashing, went thundering away through the farther scrub and disappeared, the sound of his plunging canter presently dying away. Grimwood had missed, even if he had wounded.

They camped, and all next day, leaving the canoe behind, they followed the huge track. But though they found signs of blood, these were not plentiful. The shot had evidently only grazed the big beast. The traveling was of the hardest. Toward evening, utterly exhausted, the spoor led them to the ridge they now stood upon, gazing down into the enchanting valley that opened at their feet. The giant moose had gone down into this valley. He would consider himself safe there. Grimwood agreed with the Indian's judgment. They would camp for the night and continue at dawn the wild hunt after "the biggest moose in the world."

Supper was over, the small fire used for cooking dying down, when Grimwood became first aware that the Indian was not behaving quite as usual. What particular detail drew his attention is hard to say. He was a slow-witted, heavy man, full-blooded, unobservant; a fact had to hurt him through his comfort, through his pleasure, before he noticed it. Yet anyone else must have observed the changed mood of the Redskin long ago. Tooshalli had made the fire, fried the bacon, served the tea, and was arranging the blankets, his own and his employer's, before the latter remarked upon his —silence. Tooshalli had not uttered a word for over an hour and a half, since he had first set eyes upon the new valley, to be exact. And his employer now noticed the unaccustomed silence, because after food he liked to listen to wood talk and hunting lore.

"Tired out, aren't you?" said big Grimwood, looking into the dark face across the firelight. He resented the absence of conversation, now that he noticed it. He was overweary himself, and he felt more irritable than usual, though his temper was always vile.

"Lost your tongue, eh?" he went on with a growl, as the Indian returned his stare with solemn, expressionless face. That dark inscrutable look got on his nerves a bit. "Speak up, man!" he exclaimed sharply. "What's it all about?"

The Englishman had at last realized that there was something to "speak up" about. The discovery, in his present state, annoyed him further. Tooshalli stared gravely, but made no reply. The silence was prolonged almost into minutes. Presently the head turned sideways, as though the man listened. The other watched him very closely, anger growing in him.

But it was the way the Redskin turned his head, body rigid, that gave the jerk to Grimwood's nerves, providing him with a sensation he had never known in his life before—it gave him what is generally called "the goose-flesh." It seemed to jangle his entire system, yet at the same time made him cautious. He did not like it. These emotions puzzled him.

"Say something, I tell you," he repeated in a harsher tone, raising his voice. He sat up, drawing his great body closer to the fire. "Say something!"

But his voice fell dead against the wall of surrounding trees, making the silence of the forest unpleasantly noticeable. The October air had a frosty touch that nipped.

The Redskin did not answer. No muscle of his neck nor of his stiffened body moved. He seemed all ears.

"Well?" repeated the Englishman, lowering his voice this time instinctively. "What d'you hear?"

Tooshalli slowly turned his head back again to its normal position, the body rigid as before.

"I hear nothing, Mr. Grimwood," he said, gazing with quiet dignity into his employer's eyes.

This was too much for the other, a man of savage temper at the best of times. He was the type of Englishman who held strong views as to the right way of treating "inferior" races.

"That's a lie, Tooshalli, and I won't have you lie to me. Now what was it? Tell me at once!"

"I hear nothing," repeated the other. "I only think."

"And what is it you're pleased to think?" Impatience made a nasty expression round the mouth.

"I go not," was the abrupt reply, unalterable decision in the voice.

The man's rejoinder was so unexpected that Grimwood found nothing to say at first. For a moment he did not take in its meaning. His mind, always slow, was confused by impatience, also by what he considered the foolishness of the little scene. Then in a flash he understood; but he also understood the immovable obstinacy of the race he had to deal with. Tooshalli was informing him that he refused to go into the valley where the big moose had vanished. And his astonishment was so great at first that he merely sat and stared. No words came to him.

"It is——" said the Indian, but used a native term.

"What's that mean?" Grimwood found his tongue, but his quiet tone was ominous.

"Mr. Grimwood, it mean the 'Valley of the Beasts,'" was the reply in a tone quieter still.

The Englishman made a great, a genuine effort at self-control. He was dealing, he forced himself to remember, with a superstitious Redskin. He knew the stubbornness of the type. If the man left him, his sport was irretrievably spoiled, for he could not hunt in this wilderness alone, and even if he got the coveted head, he could never, never get it out alone. His native selfishness seconded his effort. Persuasion, if only he could keep back his rising anger, was his rôle to play.

"The Valley of the Beasts," he said, a smile on his lips rather than in his darkening eyes. "But that's just what we want. It's beasts we're after, isn't it?" His voice had a false cheery ring that could not have deceived a child. "But what d'you mean, anyhow—the Valley of the Beasts?" He asked it with a dull attempt at sympathy.

"It belong to Ishtot, Mr. Grimwood." The man looked him full in the face, no flinching in the eyes.

"My—our—big moose is there," said the other, who recognized the name of the Indian Hunting God, and understanding better, felt confident he would soon persuade his man. Tooshalli, he remembered, too, was nominally a Christian. "We'll follow him at dawn and get the biggest head the world has ever seen. You will be famous," he added, his temper better in hand again. "Your tribe will honor you. And the white hunters will pay you much money."

"He go there to save himself. I go not."

The other's anger revived with a leap at this stupid obstinacy. But, in spite of it, he noticed the odd choice of words. He began to realize that nothing now would move the man. At the same time he also realized that violence on his part must prove worse than useless. Yet violence was natural to his "dominant" type. "That brute Grimwood" was the way most men spoke of him.

"Back at the settlement you're a Christian, remember," he tried, in his clumsy way, another line. "And disobedience means hell-fire. You know that!"

"I a Christian—at the post," was the reply, "but out here the Red God rule. Ishtot keep that valley for himself. No Indian hunt there." It was as though a granite boulder spoke.

The savage temper of the Englishman, enforced by the long difficult suppression, rose wickedly into sudden flame. He stood up, kicking his blankets aside. He strode across the dying fire to the Indian's side. Tooshalli also rose. They faced each other, two humans alone in the wilderness, watched by countless invisible forest eyes.

Tooshalli stood motionless, yet as though he expected

violence from the foolish, ignorant white-face. "You go alone, Mr. Grimwood." There was no fear in him.

Grimwood choked with rage. His words came forth with difficulty, though he roared them into the silence of the forest:

"I pay you, don't I? You'll do what *I* say, not what *you* say!" His voice woke the echoes.

The Indian, arms hanging by his side, gave the old reply.

"I go not," he repeated firmly.

It stung the other into uncontrollable fury. The beast then came uppermost. "You've said that once too often, Too-shalli!" and he struck him brutally in the face. The Indian fell, rose to his knees again, collapsed sideways beside the fire, then struggled back into a sitting position. He never once took his eyes from the white man's face.

Beside himself with anger, Grimwood stood over him. "Is that enough? Will you obey me now?" he shouted.

"I go not," came the thick reply, blood streaming from his mouth. The eyes had no flinching in them. "That valley Ishtot keep. Ishtot see us now. *He see you.*" The last words he uttered with strange, almost uncanny emphasis.

Grimwood, arm raised, fist clenched, about to repeat his terrible assault, paused suddenly. His arm sank to his side. What exactly stopped him he could never say. For one thing, he feared his own anger, feared that if he let himself go he would not stop till he had killed—committed murder. He knew his own fearful temper and stood afraid of it. Yet it was not only that. The calm firmness of the Redskin, his courage under pain, and something in the fixed and burning eyes arrested him. Was it also something in the words he had used—"Ishtot see *you*"—that stung him into a queer caution midway in his violence?

He could not say. He only knew that a momentary sense of awe came over him. He became unpleasantly aware of the enveloping forest, so still, listening in a kind of impenetrable, remorseless silence. This lonely wilderness, looking silently up-on what might easily prove murder, laid a faint, inexplicable chill upon his raging blood. The hand dropped slowly to his side again, the fist unclenched itself, his breath came more evenly.

"Look you here," he said, adopting without knowing it the local way of speech. "I ain't a bad man, though your going-on do make a man mad. I'll give you another chance." His voice was sullen, but a new note in it surprised even himself. "I'll do that. You can have the night to think it over, Too-shalli—see? Talk it over with your—"

He did not finish the sentence. Somehow the name of the Redskin God refused to pass his lips. He turned away, flung himself into his blankets, and in less than ten minutes, ex-hausted as much by his anger as by the day's hard going, he was sound asleep.

The Indian, crouching beside the dying fire, had said nothing.

Night held the woods, the sky was thick with stars, the life of the forest went about its business quietly, with that wondrous skill which millions of years have perfected. The Redskin, so close to this skill that he instinctively used and borrowed from it, was silent, alert and wise, his outline as in-conspicuous as though he merged, like his four-footed teachers, into the mass of the surrounding bush.

He moved perhaps, yet nothing knew he moved. His wis-dom, derived from that eternal, ancient mother who from infinite experience makes no mistakes, did not fail him. His soft tread made no sound; his breathing, like his weight, was calculated. The stars observed him, but they did not tell; the light air knew his whereabouts, yet without betrayal. . . .

The chill dawn gleamed at length between the trees, light-ing the pale ashes of an extinguished fire, also of a bulky obvious form beneath a blanket. The form moved clumsily. The cold was penetrating.

And that bulky form now moved because a dream had come to trouble it. A dark figure stole across its confused field of vision. The form started, but it did not wake. The figure spoke. "Take this," it whispered, handing over a little stick, curiously carved. "It is the totem of great Ishtot. In the valley all memory of the White Gods will leave you. Call upon Ishtot. . . . Call on him if you dare." And the dark figure glided away out of the dream and out of all remembrance. . . .

The first thing Grimwood noticed when he woke was that Tooshalli was not there. No fire burned, no tea was ready. He felt exceedingly annoyed. He glared about him, then got up with a curse to make the fire. His mind seemed confused and troubled. At first he realized only one thing clearly—his guide had left him in the night.

It was very cold. He lit the wood with difficulty and made his tea, and the actual world came gradually back to him. The Red Indian had gone. Perhaps the blow, perhaps the superstitious terror, perhaps both, had driven him away. He was alone, that was the outstanding fact.

It was while he was packing his blankets—he did it automatically, a dull, vicious resentment in him—that his fingers struck a bit of wood. He was about to throw it away when its unusual shape caught his attention suddenly. His odd dream came back then. But was it a dream? The bit of wood was undoubtedly a totem stick. He examined it. He paid it more attention than he meant to, wished to. Yes, it was unquestionably a totem stick. The dream, then, was not a dream. Tooshalli had quit, but, following with Redskin faithfulness some code of his own, had left him the means of safety. He chuckled sourly, but thrust the stick inside his belt. "One never knows," he mumbled to himself.

He faced the situation squarely. He was alone in the wilderness. His capable, experienced woodsman had deserted him. The situation was serious. What should he do? A weakling would certainly retrace his steps, following the track they had made, afraid to be left alone in the vast hinterland of pathless forest. But Grimwood was of yet another build. Alarmed he might be, but he would not give in. He had the defects of his own qualities. The brutality of his nature argued force. He was determined and a sportsman. He would go on. And ten minutes after breakfast, having first made a *cache* of what provisions were left over, he was on his way—down across the ridge and into the mysterious valley, the Valley of the Beasts.

It looked, in the morning sunlight, entrancing. The trees closed in behind him, but he did not notice. It led him on. . . .

He followed the track of the gigantic moose he meant to kill, and the sweet, delicious sunshine helped him. The air was like wine, the seductive spoor of the great beast, with here and there a faint splash of blood on leaves or ground, lay forever just before his eyes. He found the valley enticing. More and more he noticed the beauty, the desolate grandeur of the mighty spruce and hemlock, the splendor of the granite bluffs which in places rose above the forest and caught the sun. . . . The valley was deeper, vaster than he had imagined. He felt safe, at home in it, though these actual terms did not occur to him. . . . Here he could hide forever and find peace. . . . He became aware of a new quality in the deep loneliness. The scenery for the first time in his life appealed to him, and the form of the appeal was curious—he felt the comfort of it.

For a man of his habit, this was odd. Yet the new sensations stole over him so gently that they were first recognized by his consciousness indirectly. And the indirectness took this form—that the passion of the chase gave place to an interest in the valley itself. The lust of the hunt, the fierce desire to find and kill, the keen wish, in a word, to see his quarry within range, to aim, to fire, to witness the natural consummation of the long expedition—these had all become measurably less, while the effect of the valley upon him had increased in strength. There was a welcome about it that he did not understand.

The change was singular, yet it did not occur to him as singular; it was unnatural, yet it did not strike him so. To a mind of his type, a change had to be marked and dramatic before he noticed it; something in the nature of a shock must accompany it for him to recognize it had happened. And there had been no shock. The spoor of the great moose was much cleaner, now that he caught up with the animal that made it; the blood more frequent. He had noticed the spot where it had rested, its huge body leaving a marked imprint on the soft ground; where it had reached up to eat the leaves of saplings here and there was also visible. He had come undoubtedly very near to it, and any minute now might see its great bulk within range of an easy shot. Yet his ardor had somehow lessened.

He first realized this change in himself when it suddenly occurred to him that the animal itself had grown less cautious. It must scent him easily now, since a moose, its sight being indifferent, depends chiefly for its safety upon its unusually keen sense of smell, and the wind came from behind him. This now struck him as decidedly uncommon: the moose itself was obviously careless of his close approach. It felt no fear.

It was this inexplicable alteration in the animal's behavior that made him recognize, at last, the alteration in his own. He had followed it now for a couple of hours and had descended some eight hundred to a thousand feet. The trees were thinner and more sparsely placed. There were open, parklike places where silver birch, sumach and maple splashed their blazing colors; and a crystal stream, broken by many waterfalls, foamed past toward the bed of the great valley, yet another thousand feet below.

By a quiet pool against some over-arching rocks, the moose had evidently paused to drink, paused at its leisure, moreover. Grimwood, rising from a close examination of the direction the creature had taken after drinking—the hoof-marks were fresh and very distinct in the marshy ground about the pool —looked suddenly straight into the great creature's eyes. It was not twenty yards from where he stood, yet he had been standing on that spot for at least ten minutes, caught by the wonder and loneliness of the scene. The moose, therefore, had been close beside him all this time. It had been calmly drinking, undisturbed by his presence, unafraid.

The shock came now, the shock that woke his heavy nature into realization. For some seconds, probably for minutes, he stood rooted to the ground, motionless, hardly breathing. He stared as though he saw a vision. The animal's head was lowered, but turned obliquely somewhat, so that the eyes, placed sideways in its great head, could see him properly. Its immense proboscis hung as though stuffed upon an English wall. He saw the forefeet planted wide apart, the slope of the enormous shoulders dropping back toward the fine hind-quarters and lean flanks. It was a magnificent bull. The horns and head justified his wildest expectations, they were superb, a record specimen, and a phrase—where had he heard it?— ran vaguely, as from far distance, through his mind: "the biggest moose in the world."

There was the extraordinary fact, however, that he did not shoot; nor feel the wish to shoot. The familiar instinct, so strong hitherto in his blood, made no sign. The desire to kill apparently had left him. To raise his rifle, aim and fire had become suddenly an absolute impossibility.

He did not move. The animal and the human stared into each other's eyes for a length of time whose interval he could not measure. Then came a soft noise close beside him: the rifle had slipped from his grasp and fallen with a thud into the mossy earth at his feet. And the moose for the first time now was moving. With slow, easy stride, its great weight causing a squelching sound as the feet drew out of the moist ground, it came toward him, the bulk of the shoulders giving it an appearance of swaying like a ship at sea. It reached his side, it almost touched him, the magnificent head bent low, the spread of the gigantic horns lay beneath his very eyes. He could have patted, stroked it. He saw, with a touch of pity, that blood trickled from a sore in its left shoulder, matting the thick hair. It sniffed the rifle.

Then, lifting its head and shoulders again, it sniffed the air, this time with an audible sound that shook from Grimwood's mind the last possibility that he witnessed a vision or dreamed a dream. One moment it gazed into his face, its big brown eyes shining and unafraid. Then it turned abruptly, and swung away at a speed ever rapidly increasing across the parklike spaces till it was lost finally among the dark tangle of undergrowth beyond. And the Englishman's muscles turned to paper, his paralysis passed, his legs refused to support his weight, and he sank heavily to the ground. . . .

It seems he slept, slept long and heavily. He sat up, stretched himself, yawned and rubbed his eyes. Evening was drawing in. He was aware that he felt hungry. In his pouch-like pockets he had dried meat, sugar, matches, tea, and the little billy that never left him. He would make a fire, boil some tea and eat.

But he took no steps to carry out his purpose. He sat thinking, thinking. . . . What was he thinking about? He did not know, he could not say exactly; it was more like fugitive pictures that passed across his mind. Who, and where, was he? This was the Valley of the Beasts, that he knew; he felt sure of nothing else. How long had he been here, and where had he come from, and why? The questions did not linger for their answers, almost as though his interest in them was merely automatic. He felt happy, peaceful, unafraid.

He looked about him, and the spell of this virgin forest

came upon him like a charm. Only the sound of falling water, the murmur of wind sighing among innumerable branches, broke the enveloping silence. Overhead, beyond the crests of the towering trees, a cloudless evening sky was paling into transparent orange, opal, mother of pearl. He saw buzzards soaring lazily. A scarlet tanager flashed by. Soon the owls would begin to call and darkness fall like a sweet black veil and hide all detail, while the stars sparkled in their countless thousands. . . .

A glint of something that shone upon the ground caught his eye—a smooth, polished strip of rounded metal: his rifle. And he started to his feet impulsively, yet not knowing exactly what he meant to do. At the sight of the weapon, something had leaped to life in him, then faded out, died down, and was gone again.

"I'm—I'm——" he began muttering to himself, but could not finish what he was about to say. His name had disappeared completely. "I'm in the Valley of the Beasts," he repeated in place of what he sought but could not find.

This fact, that he was in the Valley of the Beasts, seemed the only positive item of knowledge that he had. About the name something known and familiar clung, though the sequence that led up to it he could not trace. Presently, nevertheless, he rose to his feet, advanced a few steps, stooped and picked up the shining metal thing, his rifle. He examined it a moment, a feeling of dread and loathing rising in him. Then, with a convulsive movement that betrayed an intense reaction of some sort he could not comprehend, he flung the thing far from him into the foaming torrent.

He saw the great white splash it made. He also saw the same instant a large grizzly bear swing heavily along the bank not a dozen yards from where he stood. It, too, heard the splash, for it started, turned, paused a second, then changed its direction and came toward him. It came up close. Its fur brushed his body. It examined him leisurely, as the moose had done, sniffed, half rose upon its terrible hind legs, opened its mouth so that red tongue and gleaming teeth were plainly visible, then flopped back upon all fours again and swung off at a quick trot back to the bank of the torrent. He had felt its hot breath upon his face, but he had felt no fear. The monster was puzzled but not hostile. It disappeared.

"They know not——" he sought for the word "man," but could not find it. "They have never been hunted."

The words ran through his mind again and again as if perhaps he was not entirely certain of their meaning. They rose, as it were, automatically; a familiar sound lay in them somewhere. At the same time there rose feelings in him that were equally, though in another way, familiar and quite natural, feelings he had once known intimately but long since laid aside.

What were they? What was their origin? They seemed distant as the stars, yet were actually in his body, in his blood and nerves, part and parcel of his flesh. Long, long ago. . . . Oh, how long, how long?

Thinking was difficult; feeling was what he most easily and naturally managed. He could not think for long; feeling rose up and drowned the effort quickly.

That huge and awful bear—not a nerve, not a muscle quivered in him as its acrid smell rose to his nostrils, its fur brushed down his legs. Yet he was aware that somewhere there was danger, though not here. Somewhere there was attack, hostility, wicked and calculated plans against him—as against that splendid, roaming animal that had sniffed, examined, then gone its own way, satisfied. Yes, active attack, hostility and careful, cruel plans against his safety, but—not here. Here he was safe, secure, at peace. Here he was happy. Here he could roam at will, no eye cast sideways into forest depths, no ear pricked high to catch sounds not explained, no nostrils quivering to scent alarm. He felt this, but he did not think of it. He felt hungry, thirsty too.

Something prompted him now at last to act. His billy lay at his feet, and he picked it up. The matches—he carried them in a metal case whose screw top kept out all moisture —were in his hand. Gathering a few dry twigs, he stooped to light them, then suddenly drew back with the first touch of fear he had yet known.

Fire! What *was* fire? The idea was repugnant to him, it was impossible, he was afraid of fire. He flung the metal case after the rifle and saw it gleam in the last rays of sunset, then sink with a little splash beneath the water. Glancing down at his billy, he realized next that he could not make use of it either, nor of the dark dry dusty stuff he had meant to boil in water. He felt no repugnance, certainly no fear, in connection with these things, only he could not handle them, he did not need them. He had forgotten, yes, "forgotten," what they meant exactly. This strange forgetfulness was increasing in him rapidly, becoming more and more complete with every minute. Yet his thirst must be quenched.

The next moment he found himself at the water's edge. He stooped to fill his billy; paused, hesitated, examined the rushing water, then abruptly moved a few feet higher up the stream, leaving the metal can behind him. His handling of it had been oddly clumsy, his gestures awkward, even unnatural. He now flung himself down with an easy, simple motion of his entire body, lowered his face to a quiet pool he had found, and drank his fill of the cool, refreshing liquid. But, though unaware of the fact, he did not drink. He lapped.

Then, crouching where he was, he ate the meat and sugar from his pockets, lapped more water, and moved back a short distance again into the dry ground beneath the trees. But he moved this time without rising to his feet, curled his body into a comfortable position and closed his eyes again to sleep. . . . No single question now raised its head in him. He felt contentment, satisfaction only. . . .

He stirred, shook himself, opened half an eye and saw, as

he had felt already in slumber, that he was not alone. In the parklike spaces in front of him, as in the shadowed fringe of the trees at his back, there was sound and movement, the sound of stealthy feet, the movement of innumerable dark bodies. There was the pad and tread of animals, the stir of backs, of smooth and shaggy beasts in countless numbers. Upon this host fell the light of a half moon sailing high in a cloudless sky. The gleam of stars, sparkling in the clear night air like diamonds, shone reflected in hundreds of ever-shifting eyes, most of them but a few feet above the ground. The whole valley was alive.

He sat upon his haunches, staring, staring, but staring in wonder, not in fear, though the foremost of the great host were so near that he could have stretched an arm and touched them. It was an ever-moving, ever-shifting throng he gazed at, spell-bound, in the pale light of moon and stars, now fading slowly towards the approaching dawn. And the smell of the forest itself was not sweeter to him in that moment than the mingled perfume, raw, pungent, acrid, of this furry host of beautiful wild animals that moved like a sea. Nor was the gleam of the starry, phosphorescent eyes less pleasantly friendly than those happy lamps that light home-lost wanderers to cosy rooms and safety. Through the wild army, in a word, poured to him the deep comfort of the entire valley, a comfort which held both the sweetness of invitation and the welcome of some magical home-coming.

No thoughts came to him, but feeling rose in a tide of wonder and acceptance. He was in his rightful place. His nature had come home. There was this dim, vague consciousness in him that after long, futile straying in another place where uncongenial conditions had forced him to be unnatural and therefore terrible, he had returned at last where he belonged. Here, in the Valley of the Beasts, he had found peace, security and happiness. He would be—he was at last—himself.

He watched the great army of the animals; they were all about him now. He crouched upon his haunches in the center of an ever-moving circle of wild forest life. He saw great timber wolves pass to and fro, loping past him with long stride and graceful swing, their red tongues lolling out; they swarmed in hundreds. Behind, yet mingling freely with them, rolled the huge grizzlies. They gamboled, sometimes they rose and stood half upright, they were comely in their mass and power. They rolled past him so close that he could touch them. And the black bear and the brown went with them, bears beyond counting, monsters and little ones, a splendid multitude. Beyond them, the immense tribe of deer gathered in vast throngs beneath the starlit sky. Moose and caribou he saw, the mighty wapiti, and the smaller deer in their crowding thousands. He heard the sound of meeting horns, the tread of innumerable hoofs, the occasional pawing of the ground as the bigger creatures maneuvered for more space about them. A wolf, he saw, was licking gently at the shoulder of a great bull-moose that had been injured. And the tide receded, advanced again, rising and falling like a living sea whose waves were animal shapes, the inhabitants of the Valley of the Beasts.

Beneath the quiet moonlight they swayed to and fro before him. They watched him, knew him, recognized him. They made him welcome.

He was aware, moreover, of a world of smaller life that formed an under-sea, as it were, numerous under-currents rather, running in and out between the great upright legs of the larger creatures. And with this smaller world also he felt at home.

How long he sat gazing, happy in himself, secure, satisfied, contented, natural, he could not say. But it was long enough for the desire to mingle with what he saw, to know closer contact, to become one with them all—long enough for this deep blind desire to assert itself, so that at length he began to move from his mossy seat toward them, to move, moreover, as they moved, and not upright on two feet.

The moon was lower now, just sinking behind a towering cedar whose ragged crest broke its light into silvery spray.

He paused and looked about him, as he advanced slowly, aware that the host already made an opening in their ranks and that the bear even nosed the earth in front, as though to show the way that was easiest for him to follow. Then, suddenly, a lynx leaped past him into the low branches of a hemlock, and he lifted his head to admire its perfect poise. He saw in the same instant the arrival of the birds, the army of the eagles, hawks and buzzards, birds of prey—the awakening flight that just precedes the dawn.

He started. He half rose to an upright position. He knew not why he did so, knew not exactly why he started. But in the attempt to find his new, and, as it now seemed, his unaccustomed balance, one hand fell against his side and came in contact with a hard, straight thing that projected awkwardly from his clothing. He pulled it out, feeling it all over with his fingers. It was a little stick. He raised it nearer to his eyes, examined it in the light of dawn now growing swiftly, remembered, or half remembered what it was—and stood stock-still.

"The totem stick," he mumbled to himself, yet audibly, finding his speech, and finding another thing—a glint of peering memory—for the first time since entering the valley.

A shock like fire ran through his body. He straightened himself, aware that a moment before he had been crawling upon his hands and knees. It seemed that something broke in his brain, lifting a veil, flinging a shutter free. And Memory peered dreadfully through the widening gap.

"I'm—I'm Grimwood," his voice uttered, though below his breath. "Tooshalli's left me. I'm alone. . . . !"

He was aware of a sudden change in the animals surrounding him. A big, grey wolf sat three feet away, glaring into his face. At its side an enormous grizzly swayed from one foot to the other. Behind it, as if looking over its shoulder, loomed a gigantic wapiti. But dawn was nearer, the sun already close to the horizon. He saw details with sharp distinctness now. The great bear rose, balancing a moment on its massive hind-quarters, then took a step toward him, its front paws spread like arms. A huge bull-moose, lowering its horns as if about to charge, joined it. A sudden excitement ran quivering over the entire host. The distant ranks moved in a new, unpleasant way. A thousand heads were lifted, ears were pricked, a forest of muzzles pointed to the wind.

And the Englishman, beside himself suddenly with a sense of ultimate terror that saw no possible escape, stiffened and stood rigid. The horror of his position petrified him. Motionless and silent he faced the awful army of his enemies, while the white light of breaking day added fresh ghastliness to the scene which was the setting for his death in the Valley of the Beasts.

Above him crouched the hideous lynx, ready to spring the instant he sought safety in the tree. Above it again, he was aware of a thousand talons of steel, fierce hooked beaks of iron, and the angry beating of prodigious wings.

He reeled, for the grizzly touched his body with its outstretched paw; the wolf crouched just before its deadly spring. In another second he would have been torn to pieces, crushed, devoured, when terror, operating naturally as ever, released the muscles of his throat and tongue. He shouted with what he believed was his last breath on earth. It was a prayer to whatever gods there be, an anguished cry for help to heaven.

"Ishtot! Great Ishtot, help me!" his voice rang out, while his hand still clutched the forgotten totem stick.

And the Red Heaven heard him.

Grimwood that same instant was aware of a presence that, but for his terror of the beasts, must have frightened him into sheer unconsciousness. A gigantic Red Indian stood before him. Yet, while the figure rose close in front of him, causing the birds to settle and the wild animals to crouch quietly where they stood, it rose also from a great distance. It seemed to fill the entire valley with its influence, its power, its amazing majesty. In some way, moreover, that he could not understand, its vast appearance included the actual valley itself with all its trees, its running streams, its open spaces and its rocky bluffs. These marked its outline, as it were, the outline of a superhuman shape. There was a mighty bow, there was a quiver of enormous arrows, there was this Red-skin to whom they belonged.

Yet the appearance, the outline, the face and figure too— these *were* the valley; and when the voice became audible it was the valley itself that uttered the appalling words. It was the voice of trees and wind, and of running, falling water that woke the echoes in the Valley of the Beasts, as, in that same moment, the sun topped the ridge and filled the scene, the outline of the majestic figure too, with a flood of dazzling light:

"You have shed blood in this my valley. . . . *I will not save. . . . !*"

The figure melted away into the sunlit forest, merging with the new-born day. But Grimwood saw close against his face the shining teeth, hot fetid breath passed over his cheeks, a power enveloped his whole body as though a mountain crushed him. He closed his eyes. He fell. A sharp, crackling sound passed through his brain, but already unconscious, he did not hear it.

His eyes opened again, and the first thing they took in was —fire. He shrank back instinctively.

"It's all right, old man. We'll bring you round. Nothing to

be frightened about." He saw the face of Iredale looking down into his own. And behind Iredale stood Tooshalli. His face was swollen. Grimwood remembered the blow. The big man began to cry.

"Painful still, is it?" Iredale said sympathetically. "Here, swallow a little of this. It'll set you right in no time."

Grimwood gulped down the spirit. He made a violent effort to control himself, but was unable to keep the tears back. He felt no pain. It was his heart that ached, though why or wherefore, he had no idea.

"I'm all to pieces," he mumbled, ashamed yet somehow not ashamed. "My nerves are rotten. What's happened?" There was no memory in him.

"You've been hugged by a bear, old man. But no bones broken. Tooshalli saved you. He fired in the nick of time—a brave shot, for he might easily have hit you instead of the brute."

"The other brute," whispered Grimwood, as the whiskey worked in him and memory came slowly back.

He saw a lake, canoes drawn up on the shore, two tents, and figures moving. Iredale explained matters briefly, then left him to sleep a bit. Tooshalli, it appeared, traveling without rest, had reached Iredale's camping ground twenty-four hours after leaving his employer. He found it deserted, Iredale and his Indian being on the hunt. When they returned at nightfall, he had explained his presence in his brief native fashion: "He struck me and I quit. He hunt now alone in Ishtot's Valley of the Beasts. He is dead, I think."

Iredale and his guide, with Tooshalli as leader, started off then and there, but Grimwood had covered a considerable distance, though leaving an easy track to follow. It was the moose tracks and the blood that guided them. They came up with him suddenly enough—in the grip of an enormous bear. It was Tooshalli that fired.

The Indian lives now in easy circumstances, all his needs

cared for, while Grimwood, his benefactor but no longer his employer, has given up hunting. He is a quiet, easy-tempered, almost gentle sort of fellow, and people wonder rather why he hasn't married. "Just the fellow to make a good father," is what they say; "so kind, good-natured and affectionate." Over the mantlepiece hangs a totem stick. He declares it saved his soul, but what he means by the expression he has never quite explained.

The Haunted Trailer

Robert Arthur

It was inevitable, of course. Bound to happen some day. But why did it have to happen to me? What did *I do* to deserve the grief? And I was going to be married, too. I sank my last thousand into that trailer, almost. In it Monica and I were going on a honeymoon tour of the United States. We were going to see the country. I was going to write, and we were going to be happy as two turtledoves.

Ha!

Ha ha!

If you detect bitterness in that laughter, I'll tell you why I'm bitter.

Because it had to be me, Mel—for Melvin—Mason who became the first person in the world to own a haunted trailer!

Now, a haunted castle is one thing. Even an ordinary haunted house can be livable. In a castle, or a house, if there's a ghost around, you can lock yourself in the bedroom and get a little sleep. A nuisance, yes. But nothing a man couldn't put up with.

43

In a trailer, though! What are you going to do when you're sharing a trailer, even a super-de-luxe model with four built-in bunks, a breakfast nook, a complete bathroom, a radio, electric range, and easy chair, with a ghost? Where can you go to get away from it?

Ha!

Ha ha!

I've heard so much ghostly laughter the last week that I'm laughing myself that way now.

There I was. I had the trailer. I had the car to pull it, naturally. I was on my way to meet Monica in Hollywood, where she was living with an aunt from Iowa. And twelve miles west of Albany, the first night out, my brand-new, spic-and-span trailer picks up a hitch-hiking haunt!

But maybe I'd better start at the beginning. It happened this way. I bought the trailer in New England—a Custom Clipper, with chrome and tan outside trim, for $2998. I hitched it on behind my sedan and headed westward, happier than a lark when the dew's on the thorn. I'd been saving up for this day for two years, and I felt wonderful.

I took it easy, getting the feel of the trailer, and so I didn't make very good time. I crossed the Hudson just after dark, trundled through Albany in a rainstorm, and half an hour later pulled off the road into an old cowpath between two big rocks to spend the night.

The thunder was rolling back and forth overhead, and the lightning was having target practice with the trees. But I'd picked out a nice secluded spot and I made myself comfortable. I cooked up a tasty plate of beans, some coffee, and some home fries. When I had eaten I took off my shoes, slumped down in the easy chair, lit a Camel, and leaned back.

"Ah!" I said aloud. "Solid comfort. If only Monica were here, how happy we would be."

But she wasn't, so I picked up a book.

It wasn't a very good book. I must have dozed off. Maybe

I napped a couple of hours. Maybe three. Anyway, I woke with a start, the echo of a buster of a thunderbolt still rattling the willow-ware set in the china closet. My hair was standing on end from the electricity in the air.

Then the door banged open, a swirl of rain swept in, and the wind—anyway, I thought it was the wind—slammed the door to. I heard a sound like a ghost—there's no other way to describe it—of a sigh.

"Now this," said a voice, "is something like!"

I had jumped up to shut the door, and I stood there with my unread book in my hand, gaping. The wind had blown a wisp of mist into my trailer and the mist, instead of evaporating, remained there, seeming to turn slowly and to settle into shape. It got more and more solid until—

Well, you know. It was a spectre. A haunt. A homeless ghost.

The creature remained there, regarding me in a decidedly cool manner.

"Sit down, chum," it said, "and don't look so pop-eyed. You make me nervous. This is my first night indoors in fifteen years, and I wanta enjoy it."

"Who—" I stammered—"who—"

"I'm not," the spectre retorted, "a brother owl, so don't who-who at me. What do I look like?"

"You look like a ghost," I told him.

"Now you're getting smart, chum. I *am* a ghost. What *kind* of a ghost do I look like?"

I inspected it more closely. Now that the air inside my trailer had stopped eddying, it was reasonably firm of outline. It was a squat, heavy-set ghost, attired in ghostly garments that certainly never had come to it new. It wore the battered ghost of a felt hat, and a stubble of ghostly beard showed on his jowls.

"You look like a tramp ghost," I answered with distaste, and my uninvited visitor nodded.

"Just what I am, chum," he told me. "Call me Spike

Higgins. Spike for short. That was my name before it happened."

"Before what happened?" I demanded. The ghost wafted across the trailer to settle down on a bunk, where he lay down and crossed his legs, hoisting one foot encased in a battered ghost of a shoe into the air.

"Before I was amachoor enough to fall asleep riding on top of a truck, and fall off right here fifteen years ago," he told me. "Ever since I been forced to haunt this place. I wasn't no Boy Scout, so I got punished by bein' made to stay here in one spot. Me, who never stayed in one spot two nights running before!

"I been gettin' kind of tired of it the last couple of years. They wouldn't even lemme haunt a house. No, I hadda do all my haunting out in th' open, where th' wind an' rain could get at me, and every dog that went by could bark at me. Chum, you don't know what it means to me to have you pick this place to stop."

"Listen," I said firmly, "you've got to get out of here!"

The apparition yawned.

"Chum," he said, "you're the one that's trespassin', not me. This is my happy haunting ground. Did I ask you to stop here?"

"You mean," I asked between clenched teeth, "that you won't go? You're going to stay here all night?"

"Right, chum," the ghost grunted. "Gimme a call for six A. M." He closed his eyes, and began snoring in an artificial and highly insulting manner.

Then I got sore. I threw the book at him, and it bounced off the bunk without bothering him in the least. Spike Higgins opened an eye and leered at me.

"Went right through me," he chortled. "Instead of me goin' through it. Ha ha! Ha ha ha! Joke."

"You—" I yelled, in a rage. "You—stuff!"

And I slammed him with the chair cushion, which likewise

went through him without doing any damage. Spike Higgins opened both eyes and stuck out his tongue at me.

Obviously I couldn't hurt him, so I got control of myself.

"Listen," I said, craftily. "You say you are doomed to haunt this spot forever? You can't leave?"

"Forbidden to leave," Spike answered. "Why?"

"Never mind," I gritted. "You'll find out."

I snatched up my slicker and hat and scrambled out into the storm. If that ghost was doomed to remain in that spot forever, I wasn't. I got in the car, got the motor going, and backed out of there. It took a lot of maneuvering in the rain, with mud underwheel, but I made it. I got straightened out on the concrete and headed westward.

I didn't stop until I'd covered twenty miles. Then, beginning to grin as I thought of the shock the ghost of Spike Higgins must have felt when I yanked the trailer right out from under him, I parked on a stretch of old, unused road and then crawled back into the trailer again.

Inside, I slammed the door and—

Ha!

Ha ha!

Ha ha ha!

Yes, more bitter laughter. Spike Higgins was still there, sound asleep and snoring.

I muttered something under my breath. Spike Higgins opened his eyes sleepily.

"Hello," he yawned. "Been having fun?"

"Listen," I finally got it out. "I—thought—you—were—doomed — to — stay — back — there — where — I — found — you —forever!"

The apparition yawned again.

"Your mistake, chum. I didn't say I was doomed to stay. I said I was forbidden to leave. I didn't leave. You hauled me away. It's all your responsibility and I'm a free agent now."

"You're a what?"

"I'm a free agent. I can ramble as far as I please. I can take up hoboing again. You've freed me. Thanks, chum. I won't forget."

"Then—then—" I sputtered. Spike Higgins nodded.

"That's right. I've adopted you. I'm going to stick with you. We'll travel together."

"But you can't!" I cried out, aghast. "Ghosts don't travel around! They haunt houses—or cemeteries—or maybe woods. But—"

"What do you know about ghosts?" Spike Higgins' voice held sarcasm. "There's all kinds of ghosts, chum. Includin' hobo ghosts, tramp ghosts, ghosts with itchin' feet who can't stay put in one spot. Let me tell you, chum, a 'bo ghost like me ain't never had no easy time of it.

"Suppose they do give him a house to haunt? All right, he's got a roof over his head, but there he is, stuck. Houses don't move around. They don't go places. They stay in spot till they rot.

"But things are different now. You've helped bring in a new age for the brotherhood of spooks. Now a fellow can haunt a house and be on the move at the same time. He can work at his job and still see the country. These trailers are the answer to a problem that's been bafflin' the best minds in th' spirit world for thousands of years. It's the newest thing, the latest and best. Haunted trailers. I tell you, we'll probably erect a monument to you at our next meeting. The ghost of a monument, anyway."

Spike Higgins had raised up on an elbow to make his speech. Now, grimacing, he lay back.

"That's enough, chum," he muttered. "Talking uses up my essence. I'm going to merge for a while. See you in the morning."

"Merge with what?" I asked. Spike Higgins was already so dim I could hardly see him.

"Merge with the otherwhere," a faint, distant voice told me, and Spike Higgins was gone.

I waited a minute to make sure. Then I breathed a big sigh of relief. I looked at my slicker, at my wet feet, at the book on the floor, and knew it had all been a dream. I'd been walking in my sleep. Driving in it too. Having a nightmare.

I hung up the slicker, slid out of my clothes, and got into a bunk.

I woke up late, and for a moment felt panic. Then I breathed easily again. The other bunk was untenanted. Whistling, I jumped up, showered, dressed, ate, and got under way.

It was a swell day. Blue sky, wind, sunshine, birds singing. Thinking of Monica, I almost sang with them as I rolled down the road. In a week I'd be pulling up in front of Monica's aunt's place in Hollywood and tooting the horn—

That was the moment when a cold draft of air sighed along the back of my neck, and the short hairs rose.

I turned, almost smacking into a hay wagon. Beside me was a misty figure.

"I got tired of riding back there alone," Spike Higgins told me. "I'm gonna ride up front a while an' look at th' scenery."

"You—you—" I shook with rage so that we nearly ran off the road. Spike Higgins reached out, grabbed the wheel in tenuous fingers, and jerked us back onto our course again.

"Take it easy, chum," he said. "There's enough competition in this world I'm in, without you hornin' into th' racket."

I didn't say anything, but my thoughts must have been written on my face. I'd thought he was just a nightmare. But he was real. A ghost had moved in on me, and I hadn't the faintest idea how to move him out.

Spike Higgins grinned with a trace of malice.

"Sure, chum," he said. "It's perfectly logical. There's

haunted castles, haunted palaces, and haunted houses. Why not a haunted trailer?"

"Why not haunted ferryboats?" I demanded with bitterness. "Why not haunted Pullmans? Why not haunted boxcars?"

"You think there ain't?" Spike Higgins' misty countenance registered surprise at my ignorance. "Could I tell you tales! There's a haunted ferryboat makes the crossing at Pough-keepsie every stormy night at midnight. There's a haunted private car on the Atchison, Santa Fé. Pal of mine haunts it. He always rode the rods, but he was a square dealer, and they gave him the private car for a reward."

"Then there's a boxcar on the New York Central that never gets where it's going. Never has yet. No matter where it starts out for, it winds up some place else. Bunch of my buddies haunt it. And another boxcar on the Southern Pacific that never has a train to pull it. Runs by itself. It's driven I dunno how many dispatchers crazy, when they saw it go past right ahead of a limited. I could tell you—"

"Don't!" I ordered. "I forbid you to. I don't want to hear."

"Why, sure, chum," Spike Higgins agreed. "But you'll get used to it. You'll be seein' a lot of me. Because where thou ghost, I ghost. Pun." He gave a ghostly chuckle and relapsed into silence. I drove along, my mind churning. I had to get rid of him. *Had* to. Before we reached California, at the very latest. But I didn't have the faintest idea in the world how I was going to.

Then, abruptly, Spike Higgins' ghost sat up straight.

"Stop!" he ordered. "Stop, I say!"

We were on a lonely stretch of road, bordered by old cypresses, with weed-grown marshland beyond. I didn't see any reason for stopping. But Spike Higgins reached out and switched off the ignition key. Then he slammed on the emergency brake. We came squealing to a stop, and just missed going into a ditch.

"What did you do that for?" I yelled. "You almost ditched us! Confound you, you ectoplasmic, hitch-hiking nuisance! If I ever find a way to lay hands on you—"

"Quiet, chum!" the apparition told me rudely. "I just seen an old pal of mine. Slippery Samuels. I ain't seen him since he dropped a bottle of nitro just as he was gonna break into a bank in Mobile sixteen years ago. We're gonna give him a ride."

"We certainly are not!" I cried. "This is my car, and I'm not picking up any more—"

"It may be your car," Spike Higgins sneered, "but I'm the resident haunt, and I got full powers to extend hospitality to any buddy ghosts I want, see? Rule 11, subdivision c. Look it up. Hey, Slippery, climb in!"

A finger of fog pushed through the partly open window of the car at his hail, enlarged, and there was a second apparition in the front seat with me.

The newcomer was long and lean, just as shabbily dressed as Spike Higgins, with a ghostly countenance as mournful as a Sunday School picnic on a rainy day.

"Spike, you old son of a gun," the second spook murmured, in hollow tones that would have brought gooseflesh to a statue. "How've you been? What're you doing here? Who's he?"—nodding at me.

"Never mind him," Spike said disdainfully. "I'm haunting his trailer. Listen, whatever became of the old gang?"

"Still 'boing it," the long, lean apparition sighed. "Nitro Nelson is somewhere around. Pacific Pete and Buffalo Benny are lying over in a haunted jungle some place near Toledo. I had a date to join 'em, but a storm blew me back to Wheeling a couple days ago."

"Mmm," Spike Higgins' ghost muttered. "Maybe we'll run into 'em. Let's go back in my trailer and do a little chinning. As for you, chum, make camp any time you want. Ta ta."

The two apparitions oozed through the back of the coupé and were gone. I was boiling inside, but there was nothing I could do.

I drove on for another hour, went through Toledo, then stopped at a wayside camp. I paid my dollar, picked out a spot, and parked.

But when I entered the trailer, the ghosts of Spike Higgins and Slippery Samuels, the bank robber, weren't there. Nor had they shown up by the time I finished dinner. In fact I ate, washed, and got into bed with no sign of them.

Breathing a prayer that maybe Higgins had abandoned me to go back to 'boing it in the spirit world, I fell asleep. And began to dream. About Monica—

When I woke, there was a sickly smell in the air, and the heavy staleness of old tobacco smoke.

I opened my eyes. Luckily, I opened them prepared for the worst. Even so, I wasn't prepared well enough.

Spike Higgins was back. Ha! Ha ha! Ha ha ha! I'll say he was back. He lay on the opposite bunk, his eyes shut, his mouth open, snoring. Just the ghost of a snore, but quite loud enough. On the bunk above him lay his bank-robber companion. In the easy chair was slumped a third apparition, short and stout, with a round, whiskered face. A tramp spirit, too.

So was the ghost stretched out on the floor, gaunt and cadaverous. So was the small, mournful spook in the bunk above me, his ectoplasmic hand swinging over the side, almost in my face. Tramps, all of them. Hobo spooks. Five hobo phantoms asleep in my trailer!

And there were cigarette butts in all the ash trays, and burns on my built-in writing desk. The cigarettes apparently had just been lit and let burn. The air was choking with stale smoke, and I had a headache I could have sold for a fire alarm, it was ringing so loudly in my skull.

I knew what had happened. During the night Spike Higgins

and his pal had rounded up some more of their ex-hobo companions. Brought them back. To *my* trailer. Now—I was so angry I saw all five of them through a red haze that gave their ectoplasm a ruby tinge. Then I got hold of myself. I couldn't throw them out. I couldn't harm them. I couldn't touch them.

No, there was only one thing I could do. Admit I was beaten. Take my loss and quit while I could. It was a bitter pill to swallow. But if I wanted to reach Monica, if I wanted to enjoy the honeymoon we'd planned, I'd have to give up the fight.

I got into my clothes. Quietly I sneaked out, locking the trailer behind me. Then I hunted up the owner of the trailer camp, a lanky man, hard-eyed, but well dressed. I figured he must have money.

"Had sort of a party last night, hey?" he asked me, with a leering wink. "I seen lights, an' heard singing, long after midnight. Not loud, though, so I didn't bother you. But it looked like somebody was havin' a high old time."

I gritted my teeth.

"That was me," I said, "I couldn't sleep. I got up and turned on the radio. Truth is, I haven't slept a single night in that trailer. I guess I wasn't built for trailer life. That job cost me $2998 new, just three days ago. I've got the bill-of-sale. How'd you like to buy it for fifteen hundred, and make two hundred easy profit on it?"

He gnawed his lip, but knew the trailer was a bargain. We settled for thirteen-fifty. I gave him the bill-of-sale, took the money, uncoupled, got into the coupé, and left there.

As I turned the bend in the road, heading westward, there was no sign that Spike Higgins' ghost was aware of what had happened.

I even managed to grin as I thought of his rage when he woke up to find I had abandoned him. It was almost worth the money I'd lost to think of it.

Beginning to feel better, I stepped on the throttle, piling up miles between me and that trailer. At least I was through with Spike Higgins and his friends.

Ha!

Ha ha!

Ha ha ha!

That's what I thought.

Along toward the middle of the afternoon I was well into Illinois. It was open country, and monotonous, so I turned on my radio. And the first thing I got was a police broadcast.

"All police, Indiana and Illinois! Be on the watch for a tan-and-chrome trailer, stolen about noon from a camp near Toledo. The thieves are believed heading west in it. That is all."

I gulped. It couldn't be! But—It sounded like my trailer, all right. I looked in my rear-vision mirror, apprehensively. The road behind was empty. I breathed a small sigh of relief. I breathed it too soon. For at that moment, around a curve half a mile behind me, something swung into sight and came racing down the road after me.

The trailer.

Ha!

Ha ha!

There it came, a tan streak that zipped around the curve and came streaking after me, zigzagging wildly from side to side of the road, making at least sixty—without any car pulling it!

My flesh crawled, and my hair stood on end. I stepped on the throttle. Hard. And I picked up speed in a hurry. In a half minute I was doing seventy, and the trailer was still gaining. Then I hit eighty—and passed a motorcycle cop parked beside the road.

I had just a glimpse of his pop-eyed astonishment as I whizzed past, with the trailer chasing me fifty yards behind. Then, kicking on his starter, he slammed after us.

Meanwhile, in spite of everything the car would do, the trailer pulled up behind me and I heard the coupling clank as it was hitched on. At once my speed dropped. The trailer was swerving dangerously, and I had to slow. Behind me the cop was coming, siren open wide, but I didn't have to worry about him because Spike Higgins was materializing beside me.

"Whew!" he said, grinning at me. "My essence feels all used up. Thought you could give Spike Higgins and his pals the slip, huh? You'll learn, chum, you'll learn. That trooper looks like a tough baby. You'll have fun trying to talk yourself out of this."

"Yes, but see what it'll get *you,* you ectoplasmic excrescence!" I raged at him. "The trailer will be stored away in some county garage for months, as evidence while I'm being held for trial on the charge of stealing it. And how'll you like haunting a garage?"

Higgins' face changed.

"Say, that's right," he muttered. "My first trip in fifteen years, too."

He put his fingers to his lips, and blew the shrill ghost of a whistle. In a moment the coupé was filled with cold, clammy drafts as Slippery Samuels and the other three apparitions appeared in the seat beside Higgins.

Twisting and turning and seeming to intermingle a lot, they peered out at the cop, who was beside the car now, one hand on his gun butt, trying to crowd me over to the shoulder.

"All right, boys!" Higgins finished explaining. "You know what we gotta do. Me an' Slippery'll take the car. You guys take the trailer."

They slipped through the open windows like smoke. Then I saw Slippery Samuels holding to the left front fender, and Spike Higgins holding to the right, their ectoplasm streaming out horizontal to the road, stretched and thinned by the air rush. And an instant later we began to move with a speed I had never dreamed of reaching.

We zipped ahead of the astonished cop, and the speedometer needle began to climb again. It took the trooper an instant to believe his eyes. Then with a yell he yanked out his gun and fired. A bullet bumbled past; then he was too busy trying to overtake us again to shoot.

The speedometer said ninety now, and was still climbing. It touched a hundred and stuck there. I was trying to pray when down the road a mile I saw a sharp curve, a bridge, and a deep river. I froze. I couldn't even yell.

We came up to the curve so fast that I was still trying to move my lips when we hit it. I didn't make any effort to take it. Instead I slammed on the brakes and prepared to plow straight ahead into a fence, a stand of young poplars, and the river.

But just as I braked, I heard Spike Higgins' ghostly scream, "Allay-OOP!"

And before we reached the ditch, car and trailer swooped up in the air. An instant later at a height of a hundred and fifty feet, we hurtled straight westward over the river and the town beyond.

I'd like to have seen the expression on the face of the motorcycle cop then. As far as that goes, I'd like to have seen my own.

Then the river was behind us, and the town, and we were swooping down toward a dank, gloomy-looking patch of woods through which ran an abandoned railway spur. A moment later we struck earth with a jouncing shock and came to rest.

Spike Higgins and Slippery Slim let go the fenders and straightened themselves up. Spike Higgins dusted ghostly dust off his palms and leered at me.

"How was that, chum?" he asked. "Neat, hey?"

"How—" I stuttered—"how—"

"Simple," Spike Higgins answered. "Anybody that can tip tables can do it. Just levitation, 'at's all. Hey, meet the boys.

You ain't been introduced yet. This is Buffalo Benny, this one is Toledo Ike, this one Pacific Pete."

The fat spook, the cadaverous one, and the melancholy little one appeared from behind the car, and smirked as Higgins introduced them. Then Higgins waved a hand impatiently.

"C'm on, chum," he said. "There's a road there that takes us out of these woods. Let's get going. It's almost dark, and we don't wanna spend the night here. This used to be in Dan Bracer's territory."

"Who's Dan Bracer?" I demanded, getting the motor going, because I was as anxious to get away from there as Spike Higgins' spook seemed to be.

"Just a railroad dick," Spike Higgins said, with a distinctly uneasy grin. "Toughest bull that ever kicked a poor 'bo off a freight."

"So mean he always drunk black coffee," Slippery Samuels put in, in a mournful voice. "Cream turned sour when he picked up the pitcher."

"Not that we was afraid of him—" Buffalo Benny, the fat apparition, squeaked. "But—"

"We just never liked him," Toledo Ike croaked, a sickly look on his ghostly features. "O' course, he ain't active now. He was retired a couple years back, an' jes' lately I got a rumor he was sick."

"Dyin'," Pacific Pete murmured hollowly.

"Dyin'." They all sighed the word, looking apprehensive. Then Spike Higgins' ghost scowled truculently at me.

"Never mind about Dan Bracer," he snapped. "Let's just get goin' out of here. And don't give that cop no more thought. You think a cop is gonna turn in a report that a car and trailer he was chasin' suddenly sailed up in the air an' flew away like a airplane? Not on your sweet life. He ain't gonna say nothing to nobody about it."

Apparently he was right, because after I had gotten out of the woods, with some difficulty, and onto a secondary highway, there was no further sign of pursuit. I headed westward again, and Spike Higgins and his pals moved back to the trailer, where they lolled about, letting my cigarettes burn and threatening to call the attention of the police to me when I complained.

I grew steadily more morose and desperate as the Pacific Coast, and Monica, came nearer. I was behind schedule, due to Spike Higgins' insistence on my taking a roundabout route so they could see the Grand Canyon, and no way to rid myself of the obnoxious haunts appeared. I couldn't even abandon the trailer. Spike Higgins had been definite on that point. It was better to haul a haunted trailer around than to have one chasing you, he pointed out, and shuddering at the thought of being pursued by a trailer full of ghosts wherever I went, I agreed.

But if I couldn't get rid of them, it meant no Monica, no marriage, no honeymoon. And I was determined that nothing as insubstantial as a spirit was going to interfere with my life's happiness.

Just the same, by the time I had gotten over the mountains and into California, I was almost on the point of doing something desperate. Apparently sensing this, Spike Higgins and the others had been on their good behavior. But I could still see no way to get rid of them.

It was early afternoon when I finally rolled into Hollywood, haggard and unshaven, and found a trailer camp, where I parked. Heavy-hearted, I bathed and shaved and put on clean clothes. I didn't know what I was going to say to Monica, but I was already several days behind schedule, and I couldn't put off calling her.

There was a pay phone in the camp office. I looked up Ida Bracer—her aunt's name—in the book, then put through the call.

Monica herself answered. Her voice sounded distraught.

"Oh, Mel," she exclaimed, as soon as I announced myself,

"where have you been? I've been expecting you for just days."

"I was delayed," I told her, bitterly. "Spirits. I'll explain later."

"Spirits?" Her tone seemed cold. "Well, anyway, now that you're here at last, I must see you at once. Mel, Uncle Dan is dying."

"Uncle Dan?" I echoed.

"Yes, Aunt Ida's brother. He used to live in Iowa, but a few months ago he was taken ill, and he came out to be with Aunt and me. Now he's dying. The doctor says it's only a matter of hours."

"Dying?" I repeated again. "Your Uncle Dan, from Iowa, dying?"

Then it came to me. I began to laugh. Exultantly.

"I'll be right over!" I said, and hung up.

Still chuckling, I hurried out and unhitched my car. Spike Higgins stared at me suspiciously.

"Just got an errand to do," I said airily. "Be back soon."

"You better be," Spike Higgins' ghost said. "We wanta drive around and see these movie stars' houses later on."

Ten minutes later Monica herself, trim and lovely, was opening the door for me. In high spirits, I grabbed her around the waist, and kissed her. She turned her cheek to me, then, releasing herself, looked at me strangely.

"Mel," she frowned, "what in the world is wrong with you?"

"Nothing," I caroled. "Monica darling, I've got to talk to your uncle."

"But he's too sick to see anyone. He's sinking fast, the doctor says."

"All the more reason why I must see him," I told her, and pushed into the house. "Where is he, upstairs?"

I hurried up, and into the sickroom. Monica's uncle, a big man with a rugged face and a chin like the prow of a battleship, was in bed, breathing stertorously.

"Mr. Bracer!" I said, breathless, and his eyes opened slowly.

"Who're you?" a voice as raspy as a shovel scraping a concrete floor growled.

"I'm going to marry Monica," I told him. "Mr. Bracer, have you ever heard of Spike Higgins? Or Slippery Samuels? Or Buffalo Benny, Pacific Pete, Toledo Ike?"

"Heard of 'em?" A bright glow came into the sick man's eyes. "Ha! I'll say I have. And laid hands on 'em, too, more'n once. But they're dead now."

"I know they are," I told him. "But they're still around. Mr. Bracer, how'd you like to meet up with them again?"

"Would I!" Dan Bracer murmured, and his hands clenched in unconscious anticipation. "Ha!"

"Then," I said, "if you'll wait for me in the cemetery the first night after—after—well, anyway, wait for me, and I'll put you in touch with them."

The ex-railroad detective nodded. He grinned broadly, like a tiger viewing its prey, and eager to be after it. Then he lay back, his eyes closed, and Monica, running in, gave a little gasp.

"He's gone!" she said.

"Ha ha!" I chuckled. "Ha ha ha! What a surprise this is going to be to certain parties."

The funeral was held in the afternoon, two days later. I didn't see Monica much in the interim. In the first place, though she hadn't known her uncle well, and wasn't particularly grieved, there were a lot of details to be attended to. In the second place, Spike Higgins and his pals kept me on the jump. I had to drive around Hollywood, to all the stars' houses, to Malibou Beach, Santa Monica, Laurel Canyon, and the various studios, so they could rubberneck.

Then too, Monica rather seemed to be avoiding me, when I did have time free. But I was too inwardly gleeful at the prospect of getting rid of the ghosts of Higgins and his pals to notice.

I managed to slip away from Higgins to attend the funeral of Dan Bracer, but could not help grinning broadly, and even at times chuckling, as I thought of his happy anticipation of meeting Spike Higgins and the others again. Monica eyed me oddly, but I could explain later. It wasn't quite the right moment to go into details.

After the funeral, Monica said she had a headache, so I promised to come around later in the evening. I returned to the trailer to find Spike Higgins and the others sprawled out, smoking my cigarettes again. Higgins looked at me with dark suspicion.

"Chum," he said, "we wanta be hitting the road again. We leave tomorrow, get me?"

"Tonight, Spike," I said cheerfully. "Why wait? Right after sundown you'll be on your way. To distant parts. Tra la, tra le, tum tum te tum."

He scowled, but could think of no objection. I waited impatiently for sundown. As soon as it was thoroughly dark, I hitched up and drove out of the trailer camp, heading for the cemetery where Dan Bracer had been buried that afternoon.

Spike Higgins was still surly, but unsuspicious until I drew up and parked by the low stone wall at the nearest point to Monica's uncle's grave. Then, gazing out at the darkness-shadowed cemetery, he looked uneasy.

"Say," he snarled, "whatcha stoppin' here for? Come on, let's be movin'."

"In a minute, Spike," I said. "I have some business here."

I slid out and hopped over the low wall.

"Mr. Bracer!" I called. "Mr. Bracer!"

I listened, but a long freight rumbling by half a block distant, where the Union Pacific lines entered the city, drowned out any sound. For a moment I could see nothing. Then a misty figure came into view among the headstones.

"Mr. Bracer!" I called as it approached. "This way!"

The figure headed toward me. Behind me Spike Higgins,

Slippery Samuels and the rest of the ghostly crew were pressed against the wall, staring apprehensively into the darkness. And they were able to recognize the dim figure approaching before I could be sure of it.

"Dan Bracer!" Spike Higgins choked, in a high, ghostly squeal.

"It's him!" Slippery Samuels groaned.

"In the spirit!" Pacific Pete wailed. "Oh oh oh oh OH!"

They tumbled backwards, with shrill squeaks of dismay. Dan Bracer's spirit came forward faster. Paying no attention to me, he took out after the retreating five.

Higgins turned and fled, wildly, with the others at his heels. They were headed toward the railroad tracks, over which the freight was still rumbling, and Dan Bracer was now at their heels. Crowding each other, Higgins and Slippery Samuels and Buffalo Benny swung onto a passing car, with Pacific Pete and Toledo Ike catching wildly at the rungs of the next.

They drew themselves up to the top of the boxcars, and stared back. Dan Bracer's ghost seemed, for an instant, about to be left behind. But one long ectoplasmic arm shot out. A ghostly hand caught the rail of the caboose, and Dan Bracer swung aboard. A moment later, he was running forward along the tops of the boxcars, and up ahead of him, Spike Higgins and his pals were racing toward the engine.

That was the last I saw of them—five phantom figures fleeing, the sixth pursuing in happy anticipation. Then they were gone out of my life, headed east.

Still laughing to myself at the manner in which I had rid myself of Spike Higgins' ghost, and so made it possible for Monica and me to be married and enjoy our honeymoon trailer trip after all, I drove to Monica's aunt's house.

"Melvin!" Monica said sharply, as she answered my ring. "What are you laughing about now?"

"Your uncle," I chuckled. "He—"

"My uncle!" Monica gasped. "You—you fiend! You laughed

when he died! You laughed all during his funeral! Now you're laughing because he's dead!"

"No, Monica!" I said. "Let me explain. About the spirits, and how I—"

Her voice broke.

"Forcing your way into the house—laughing at my poor Uncle Dan—laughing at his funeral—"

"But Monica!" I cried. "It isn't that way at all. I've just been to the cemetery, and—"

"And came back laughing," Monica retorted. "I never want to see you again. Our engagement is broken. And worst of all is the *way* you laugh. It's so—so ghostly! So spooky. Blood-chilling. Even if you hadn't done the other things, I could never marry a man who laughs like that. So here's your ring. And good-by."

Leaving me staring at the ring in my hand, she slammed the door. And that was that. Monica is very strong-minded, and what she says, she means. I couldn't even try to explain. About Spike Higgins. And how I'd unconsciously come to laugh that way through associating with five phantoms. After all, I'd just rid myself of them for good. And the only way Monica would ever have believed my story would have been from my showing her Spike Higgins' ghost himself.

Ha!

Ha ha!

Ha ha ha ha!

If you know anyone who wants to buy a practically unused trailer, cheap, have them get in touch with me.

The Upper Berth

F. Marion Crawford

I

Somebody asked for the cigars. We had talked long, and the conversation was beginning to languish. The tobacco smoke had got into the heavy curtains, and it was already perfectly evident that, unless somebody did something to rouse our oppressed spirits, the meeting would soon come to its natural conclusion, and we, the guests, would speedily go home to bed. No one had said anything very remarkable; it may be that no one had anything very remarkable to say. Jones had given us every particular of his last hunting adventure in Yorkshire. Mr. Tompkins, of Boston, had explained at elaborate length those working principles by the due and careful maintenance of which the Atchison, Topeka, and Santa Fé Railroad not only extended its territory, but, also, had for years succeeded in deceiving passengers into the belief that the corporation aforesaid was really able to transport human life without destroying it.

It is unnecessary to go into further details. We had sat at

table for hours; we were bored, we were tired, and nobody showed signs of moving.

Somebody called for cigars. We all instinctively looked toward the speaker. Brisbane was a man of five-and-thirty years of age, and remarkable for those gifts which chiefly attract the attention of men. He was a strong man. The external proportions of his figure presented nothing extraordinary to the common eye, though his size was above the average. He was a little over six feet in height, and moderately broad in the shoulder. He did not appear to be stout, but, on the other hand, he was certainly not thin. His small head was supported by a strong and sinewy neck; his broad, muscular hands appeared to possess a peculiar skill in breaking walnuts without the assistance of the ordinary cracker. And, seeing him in profile, one could not help remarking the extraordinary breadth of his sleeves and the unusual thickness of his chest. He was one of those men who are commonly spoken of among men as deceptive; that is to say that though he looked exceedingly strong he was in reality very much stronger than he looked. Of his features I need say little. His head is small, his hair is thin, his eyes are blue, his nose is large, he has a small mustache and a square jaw. Everybody knows Brisbane, and when he asked for a cigar everybody looked at him.

"It is a very singular thing," said Brisbane.

Everybody stopped talking. Brisbane's voice was not loud, but possessed a peculiar quality of penetrating general conversation and cutting it like a knife. Everybody listened. Brisbane, perceiving that he had attracted their general attention, lighted his cigar with great equanimity.

"It is very singular," he continued, "that thing about ghosts. People are always asking whether anybody has seen a ghost. I have."

"Bosh! What, you? You don't mean to say so, Brisbane? Well, for a man of your intelligence!"

A chorus of exclamations greeted Brisbane's remarkable statement. Everybody called for cigars, and Stubbs, the butler, suddenly appeared from the depths of nowhere with a fresh bottle of dry champagne. The situation was saved; Brisbane was going to tell a story.

"I am an old sailor," said Brisbane, "and as I have to cross the Atlantic pretty often, I have my favorites. I have a habit of waiting for certain ships when I am obliged to cross that duckpond. It may be a prejudice, but I was never cheated out of a good passage but once in my life. I remember it very well. It was in June, and the 'Kamtschatka' was one of my favorite ships. I say was, because she emphatically no longer is. I cannot conceive of any inducement which could entice me to make another voyage in her. Yes, I know what you are going to say. She is uncommonly clean in the run aft, she has enough bluffing off in the bows to keep her dry, and the lower berths are most of them double. She has a lot of advantages, but I won't cross in her again. Excuse the digression. I got on board. I hailed a steward, whose red nose and redder whiskers were equally familiar to me.

"'One hundred and five, lower berth,' said I in a business-like tone.

"The steward took my portmanteau, greatcoat, and rug. I shall never forget the expression of his face. Not that he turned pale. But, from his expression, I judged that he was either about to shed tears, to sneeze, or to drop my portmanteau. As the latter contained two bottles of particularly fine old sherry presented to me for my voyage by my old friend Snigginson van Pickyns, I felt extremely nervous. But the steward did none of these things.

"'Well, I'll be blowed!' said he in a low voice, and led the way.

"I supposed the steward, as he led me to the lower regions, had had a little grog, but I said nothing, and followed him. One hundred and five was on the port side, well aft. There was nothing remarkable about the stateroom. The lower berth, like most of those upon the 'Kamtschatka,' was double. There was plenty of room. There was the usual washing apparatus, there were the usual inefficient racks of brown wood, in which it is more easy to hang a large-sized umbrella than the common toothbrush. Upon the uninviting mattresses were carefully folded together those blankets which a great modern humorist has aptly compared to cold buckwheat cakes. The question of towels was left entirely to the imagination. The glass decanters were filled with a transparent liquid faintly tinged with brown, but from which an odor less faint, but not more pleasing, ascended to the nostrils, like a far-off sea-sick reminiscence of oily machinery. Sad-colored curtains half closed the upper berth. The hazy June daylight shed a faint illumination upon the desolate little scene. Ugh! how I hate that stateroom!

"The steward deposited my traps and looked at me as though he wanted to get away—probably in search of more passengers and more fees. It is always a good plan to start in favor with those functionaries, and I accordingly gave him certain coins there and then.

"'I'll try and make yer comfortable all I can,' he remarked, as he put the coins in his pocket. Nevertheless, there was a doubtful intonation in his voice which surprised me. Possibly his scale of fees had gone up, and he was not satisfied. But on the whole I was inclined to think that, as he himself would have expressed it, he was 'the better for a glass.' I was wrong, however, and did the man injustice.

II

Nothing especially worthy of mention occurred during that day. We left the pier punctually, and it was very pleasant to be fairly under way, for the weather was warm and sultry, and the motion of the steamer produced a refreshing breeze.

"Everybody knows what the first day at sea is like. People pace the decks and stare at each other, and occasionally meet acquaintances whom they did not know to be on board. There is the usual uncertainty as to whether the food will be good, bad, or indifferent, until the first two meals have put the matter beyond a doubt. There is the usual uncertainty about the weather, until the ship is fairly off Fire Island. The tables are crowded at first, and then suddenly thinned. Pale-faced people spring from their seats and precipitate themselves toward the door, and each old sailor breathes more freely as his seasick neighbor rushes from his side, leaving him plenty of elbow room and an unlimited command over the mustard.

"One passage across the Atlantic is very much like another, and we who cross very often do not make the voyage for the sake of novelty. Whales and icebergs are indeed always objects of interest, but, after all, one whale is very much like another whale, and one rarely sees an iceberg at close quarters. To the majority of us the most delightful moment of the day on board an ocean steamer is when we have taken our last turn on deck, have smoked our last cigar, and having succeeded in tiring ourselves, feel at liberty to turn in with a clear conscience. On that first night of the voyage I felt particularly lazy, and went to bed in one hundred and five rather earlier than I usually do. As I turned in, I was amazed to see that I was to have a companion. A portmanteau, very like my own, lay in the opposite corner, and in the upper berth had been deposited a neatly folded rug with a stick and umbrella. I had hoped to be alone, and I was disappointed; but I wondered who my roommate was to be, and I determined to have a look at him.

"Before I had been long in bed he entered. He was, as far as I could see, a very tall man, very thin, very pale, with sandy hair and whiskers and colorless gray eyes. He had about him, I thought, an air of rather dubious fashion; the sort of man you might see in Wall Street, without being able precisely to say what he was doing there. A little over-dressed—a little odd. There are three or four of his kind on every ocean steamer. I made up my mind that I did not care to make his acquaintance, and I went to sleep saying to myself that I would study his habits in order to avoid him. If he rose early, I would rise late; if he went to bed late, I would go to bed early. I did not care to know him. If you once know people of that kind they are always turning up. Poor fellow! I need not have taken the trouble to come to so many decisions about him, for I never saw him again after that first night in one hundred and five.

"I was sleeping soundly when I was suddenly waked by a loud noise. To judge from the sound, my roommate must have sprung with a single leap from the upper berth to the floor. I heard him fumbling with the latch and bolt of the door, which opened almost immediately, and then I heard his footsteps as he ran at full speed down the passage, leaving the door open behind him. The ship was rolling a little, and I expected to hear him stumble or fall, but he ran as though he were running for his life. The door swung on its hinges with the motion of the vessel, and the sound annoyed me. I got up and shut it, and groped my way back to my berth in the darkness. I went to sleep again; but I have no idea how long I slept.

"When I awoke it was still quite dark, but I felt a dis-agreeable sensation of cold, and it seemed to me that the air was damp. You know the peculiar smell of a cabin which has been wet with sea water. I covered myself up as well as I could and dozed off again, framing complaints to be made the next day. I could hear my roommate turn over in the upper berth. He had probably returned while I was asleep.

Once I thought I heard him groan, and I argued that he was seasick. That is particularly unpleasant when one is below. Nevertheless I dozed off and slept till early daylight.

"The ship was rolling heavily, much more than on the previous evening, and the gray light which came in through the porthole changed in tint with every movement according as the angle of the vessel's side turned the glass seaward or skyward. It was very cold—unaccountably so for the month of June. I turned my head and looked at the porthole, and saw to my surprise that it was wide open and hooked back. I got up and shut it. As I turned back I glanced at the upper berth. The curtains were drawn close together; my companion had probably felt as cold as I. It struck me that I had slept enough. The stateroom was uncomfortable, though, strange to say, I could not smell the dampness which had annoyed me in the night. My roommate was still asleep— excellent opportunity for avoiding him, so I dressed at once and went on deck. The day was warm and cloudy, with an oily smell on the water. It was seven o'clock as I came out— much later than I had imagined. I came across the doctor, who was taking his first sniff of the morning air. He was a young man from the West of Ireland—a tremendous fellow, with black hair and blue eyes, already inclined to be stout; he had a happy-go-lucky, healthy look about him which was rather attractive.

" 'Fine mornin,' I remarked, by way of introduction.

" 'Well,' said he, eying me with an air of ready interest, 'it's a fine morning and it's not a fine morning. I don't think it's much of a morning.'

" 'Well, no—it is not so very fine,' said I.

" 'It's just what I call fuggly weather,' replied the doctor.

" 'It was very cold last night, I thought,' I remarked. 'However, when I looked about, I found that the porthole was wide open. I had not noticed it when I went to bed. And the stateroom was damp, too.'

"'Damp!' said he. 'Whereabouts are you?'

"'One hundred and five—'

"To my surprise the doctor started visibly, and stared at me.

"'What is the matter?' I asked.

"'Oh—nothing,' he answered; 'only everybody has complained of that stateroom for the last three trips.'

"'I shall complain too,' I said. 'It has certainly not been properly aired. It is a shame!'

"'I don't believe it can be helped,' answered the doctor. 'I believe there is something—well, it is not my business to frighten passengers.'

"'You need not be afraid of frightening me,' I replied. 'I can stand any amount of damp. If I should get a bad cold I will come to you.'

"I offered the doctor a cigar, which he took and examined very critically.

"'It is not so much the damp,' he remarked. 'However, I dare say you will get on very well. Have you a roommate?'

"'Yes; a deuce of a fellow, who bolts out in the middle of the night and leaves the door open.'

"Again the doctor glanced curiously at me. Then he lighted the cigar and looked grave.

"'Did he come back?' he asked presently.

"'Yes. I was asleep, but I waked up and heard him moving. Then I felt cold and went to sleep again. This morning I found the porthole open.'

"'Look here,' said the doctor, quietly, 'I don't care much for this ship. I don't care a rap for her reputation. I tell you what I will do. I have a good-sized place up here. I will share it with you, though I don't know you from Adam.'

"I was very much surprised at the proposition. I could not imagine why he should take such a sudden interest in my welfare. However, his manner as he spoke of the ship was peculiar.

"'You are very good, Doctor,' I said. 'But really, I believe even now the cabin could be aired, or cleaned out, or something. Why do you not care for the ship?'

"'We are not superstitious in our profession, sir,' replied the doctor. 'But the sea makes people so. I don't want to prejudice you, and I don't want to frighten you, but if you will take my advice you will move in here. I would as soon see you overboard,' he added, 'as know that you or any other man was to sleep in one hundred and five.'

"'Good gracious! Why?' I asked.

"'Just because on the last three trips the people who have slept there actually have gone overboard,' he answered gravely.

"The intelligence was startling and exceedingly unpleasant, I confess. I looked hard at the doctor to see whether he was making game of me, but he looked perfectly serious. I thanked him warmly for his offer, but told him I intended to be the exception to the rule by which everyone who slept in that particular stateroom went overboard. He did not say much, but looked as grave as ever, and hinted that before we got across I should probably reconsider his proposal. In the course of time we went to breakfast, at which only an inconsiderable number of passengers assembled. I noticed that one or two of the officers who breakfasted with us looked grave. After breakfast I went into my stateroom in order to get a book. The curtains of the upper berth were still closely drawn. Not a word was to be heard. My roommate was probably still asleep.

"As I came out I met the steward whose business it was to look after me. He whispered that the captain wanted to see me, and then scuttled away down the passage as if very anxious to avoid any questions. I went toward the captain's cabin, and found him waiting for me.

"'Sir,' said he, 'I want to ask a favor of you.'

"I answered that I would do anything to oblige him.

"'Your roommate has disappeared,' he said. 'He is known to have turned in early last night. Did you notice anything extraordinary in his manner?'

"The question coming, as it did, in exact confirmation of the fears the doctor had expressed half an hour earlier, staggered me.

"'You don't mean to say he has gone overboard?' I asked.

"'I fear he has,' answered the captain.

"'This is the most extraordinary thing—' I began.

"'Why?' he asked.

"'He is the fourth, then?' I exclaimed. In answer to another question from the captain, I explained, without mentioning the doctor, that I had heard the story concerning one hundred and five. He seemed very much annoyed at hearing that I knew of it. I told him what had occurred in the night.

"'What you say,' he replied, 'coincides almost exactly with what was told me by the roommates of two of the other three. They bolt out of bed and run down the passage. Two of them were seen to go overboard by the watch; we stopped and lowered boats, but they were not found. Nobody, however, saw or heard the man who was lost last night—if he is really lost. The steward, who is a superstitious fellow, perhaps, and expected something to go wrong, went to look for him this morning, and found his berth empty, but his clothes lying about, just as he had left them. The steward was the only man on board who knew him by sight, and he has been searching everywhere for him. He has disappeared! Now, sir, I want to beg you not to mention the circumstance to any of the passengers; I don't want the ship to get a bad name, and nothing hangs about an ocean-goer like stories of suicides. You shall have your choice of any one of the officers' cabins you like, including my own, for the rest of the passage. Is that a fair bargain?'

"'Very,' said I; 'and I am much obliged to you. But since I am alone, and have the stateroom to myself, I would rather not move. If the steward will take out that unfortunate man's things, I would as lief stay where I am. I will not say anything about the matter, and I think I can promise you that I will not follow my roommate.'

"The captain tried to dissuade me from my intention, but I preferred having a stateroom alone to being the chum of any officer on board. I do not know whether I acted foolishly, but if I had taken his advice I should have had nothing more to tell. There would have remained the disagreeable coincidence of several suicides occurring among men who had slept in the same cabin, but that would have been all.

"That was not the end of the matter, however, by any means. I obstinately made up my mind that I would not be disturbed by such tales, and I even went so far as to argue the question with the captain. There was something wrong about the stateroom, I said. It was rather damp. The porthole had been left open last night. My roommate might have been ill when he came on board, and he might have become delirious after he went to bed. He might even now be hiding somewhere on board, and might be found later. The place ought to be aired and the fastening of the port looked to. If the captain would give me leave, I would see that what I thought necessary was done immediately.

"'Of course you have a right to stay where you are if you please,' he replied, rather petulantly; 'but I wish you would turn out and let me lock the place up, and be done with it.'

"I did not see it in the same light, and left the captain, after promising to be silent concerning the disappearance of my companion. The latter had had no acquaintances on board, and was not missed in the course of the day. Toward evening I met the doctor again, and he asked me whether I had changed my mind. I told him I had not.

" 'Then you will before long,' he said, very gravely.

III

"We played whist in the evening, and I went to bed late. I will confess now that I felt a disagreeable sensation when I entered my stateroom. I could not help thinking of the tall man I had seen on the previous night, who was now dead, drowned, tossing about in the long swell two or three hundred miles astern. His face rose very distinctly before me as I undressed, and I even went so far as to draw back the curtains of the upper berth, as though to persuade myself that he was actually gone. I also bolted the door of the stateroom. Suddenly I became aware that the porthole was open and fastened back. This was more than I could stand. I hastily threw on my dressing-gown and went in search of Robert, the steward of my passage. I was very angry, I remember, and when I found him I dragged him roughly to the door of one hundred and five, and pushed him toward the open porthole.

" 'What the deuce do you mean, you scoundrel, by leaving that port open every night? Don't you know it is against the regulations? Don't you know that if the ship heeled and the water began to come in ten men could not shut it? I will report you to the captain, you blackguard, for endangering the ship!'

"I was exceedingly wroth. The man trembled and turned pale, and then began to shut the round glass plate with the heavy brass fittings.

" 'Why don't you answer me?' I said roughly.

" 'If you please, sir,' faltered Robert, 'there's nobody on board as can keep this 'ere port shut at night. You can try it yourself, sir. I ain't a-going to stop hany longer on board o' this vessel, sir; I ain't, indeed. But if I was you, sir, I'd just clear out and go and sleep with the surgeon or something, I would. Look 'ere, sir, is that fastened what you may call securely, or not? Try it, sir, see if it will move a hinch.'

"I tried the port, and found it perfectly tight.

"'Well, sir,' continued Robert, triumphantly, 'I wager my reputation as a AI steward that in arf an hour it will be open again; fastened back, too, sir, that's the horful thing—fastened back!'

"I examined the great screw and the looped nut that ran on it.

"'If I find it open in the night, Robert, I will give you a sovereign. It is not possible. You may go.'

"'Sovereign, did you say, sir? Very good, sir. Thank ye, sir. Good night, sir. Pleasant reepose, sir, and all manner of hinchantin' dreams, sir.'

"Robert scuttled away, delighted at being released. Of course, I thought he was trying to account for his negligence by a silly story, intended to frighten me, and I disbelieved him.

"I went to bed, and five minutes after I had rolled myself up in my blankets Robert extinguished the light that burned steadily behind the ground-glass pane near the door. I lay quite still in the dark trying to go to sleep, but I soon found that impossible. It had been some satisfaction to be angry with the steward, and the diversion had banished that unpleasant sensation I had at first experienced when I thought of the drowned man who had been my roommate. I was no longer sleepy, and I lay awake for some time, occasionally glancing at the porthole, which I could just see from where I lay, and which, in the darkness, looked like a faintly luminous soup-plate suspended in blackness. I believe I must have lain there for an hour, and, as I remember, I was just dozing into sleep when I was roused by a draught of cold air and by distinctly feeling the spray of the sea blown upon my face. I started to my feet, and not having allowed in the dark for the motion of the ship, I was instantly thrown violently across the stateroom upon the couch which was placed beneath the porthole. I recovered myself immediately, however, and climbed upon my knees. The porthole was again wide open and fastened back!

"Now these things are facts. I was wide-awake when I got up, and I should certainly have been waked by the fall had I still been dozing. Moreover, I bruised my elbows and knees badly, and the bruises were there on the following morning to testify to the fact, if I myself had doubted it. The porthole was wide open and fastened back—a thing so unaccountable that I remember very well feeling astonishment rather than fear when I discovered it. I at once closed the plate again and screwed down the loop nut with all my strength. It was very dark in the stateroom. I reflected that the port had certainly been opened within an hour after Robert had at first shut it in my presence, and I determined to watch it and see whether it would open again. Those brass fittings are very heavy and by no means easy to move; I could not believe that the clamp had been turned by the shaking of the screw. I stood peering out through the thick glass at the alternate white and gray streaks of the sea that foamed beneath the ship's side. I must have remained there a quarter of an hour.

"Suddenly, as I stood, I distinctly heard something moving behind me in one of the berths, and a moment afterward, just as I turned instinctively to look—though I could, of course, see nothing in the darkness—I heard a very faint groan. I sprang across the stateroom, and tore the curtains of the upper berth aside, thrusting in my hands to discover if there were anyone there. There was someone.

"I remember that the sensation as I put my hands forward was as though I were plunging them into the air of a damp cellar, and from behind the curtain came a gust of wind that smelled horribly of stagnant sea water. I laid hold of something that had the shape of a man's arm, but was smooth, and wet, and icy cold. But suddenly, as I pulled, the creature sprang violently forward against me, a clammy, oozy mass, as it seemed to me, heavy and wet, yet endowed with a sort of supernatural strength. I reeled across the stateroom, and in an instant the door opened and the thing rushed out.

"I had not had time to be frightened, and quickly recovering myself, I sprang through the door and gave chase at the top of my speed, but I was too late. Ten yards before me I could see—I am sure I saw it—a dark shadow moving in the dimly lighted passage, quickly as the shadow of a fast horse thrown before a dog-cart by the lamp on a dark night. But in a moment it had disappeared, and I found myself holding on to the polished rail that ran along the bulkhead where the passage turned toward the companion. My hair stood on end, and the cold perspiration rolled down my face. I am not ashamed of it in the least: I was very badly frightened.

"Still I doubted my senses, and pulled myself together. It was absurd, I thought. The Welsh rarebit I had eaten had disagreed with me. I had been in a nightmare. I made my way back to my stateroom, and entered it with an effort. The whole place smelled of stagnant sea water, as it had when I had waked on the previous evening. It required my utmost strength to go in and grope among my things for a box of wax lights. As I lighted a railway reading-lantern which I always carry in case I want to read after the lamps are out, I perceived that the porthole was again open. A sort of creeping horror began to take possession of me which I never felt before, nor wish to feel again. But I got a light and proceeded to examine the upper berth, expecting to find it drenched with sea water.

"But I was disappointed. The bed had been slept in, and the smell of the sea was strong; but the bedding was as dry as a bone. I fancied that Robert had not had the courage to make the bed after the accident of the previous night—it had all been a hideous dream. I drew the curtains back as far as I could and examined the place very carefully. It was perfectly dry. But the porthole was open again. With a sort of dull bewilderment of horror, I closed it and screwed it down, and thrusting my heavy stick through the brass loop, wrenched it with all my might, till the thick metal began to bend under the pressure. Then I hooked my reading-lantern into the red velvet at the head of the couch, and sat down to recover my senses if I could. I sat there all night, unable to think of rest—hardly able to think at all. But the porthole remained closed, and I did not believe it would now open again without the application of a considerable force.

"The morning dawned at last, and I dressed myself slowly, thinking over all that had happened in the night. It was a beautiful day and I went on deck, glad to get out in the early pure sunshine, and to smell the breeze from the blue water, so different from the stagnant odor from my stateroom. Instinctively I turned aft, toward the surgeon's cabin. There he stood with a pipe in his mouth, taking his morning airing precisely as on the preceding day.

" 'Good morning,' said he quietly, but looking at me with evident curiosity.

" 'Doctor, you were quite right,' said I. 'There is something wrong about that place.'

" 'I thought you would change your mind,' he answered, rather triumphantly. 'You have had a bad night, eh? Shall I make you a pick-me-up? I have a capital recipe.'

" 'No, thanks,' I cried. 'But I would like to tell you what happened.'

"I then tried to explain as clearly as possible precisely what had occurred, not omitting to state that I had been scared as I had never been scared in my whole life before. I dwelt particularly on the phenomenon of the porthole, which was a fact to which I could testify, even if the rest had been an illusion. I had closed it twice in the night, and the second time I had actually bent the brass in wrenching it with my stick. I believe I insisted a good deal on this point.

"'You seem to think I am likely to doubt the story,' said the doctor, smiling at the detailed account of the state of the porthole. 'I do not doubt it in the least. I renew my invitation to you. Bring your traps here, and take half my cabin.'

"'Come and take half of mine for one night,' I said. 'Help me to get at the bottom of this thing.'

"'You will get to the bottom of something else if you try,' answered the doctor.

"'What?' I asked.

"'The bottom of the sea. I am going to leave the ship. It is not canny.'

"'Then you will not help me to find out—'

"'Not I,' said the doctor, quickly. 'It is my business to keep my wits about me—not to go fiddling about with ghosts and things.'

"'Do you really believe it is a ghost?' I inquired, rather contemptuously. But as I spoke I remembered very well the horrible sensation of the supernatural which had got possession of me during the night. The doctor turned sharply on me:

"'Have you any reasonable explanation of these things to offer?' he asked. 'No; you have not. Well, you say you will find an explanation. I say that you won't, sir, simply because there is not any.'

"'But, my dear sir,' I retorted, 'do you, a man of science, mean to tell me that such things cannot be explained?"

"'I do,' he answered, stoutly. 'And if they could, I would not be concerned in the explanation.'

"I did not care to spend another night alone in the stateroom, and yet I was obstinately determined to get at the root of the disturbances. I do not believe there are many men who would have slept there alone, after passing two such nights. But I made up my mind to try it, if I could not get anyone to share a watch with me. The doctor was evidently not inclined for such an experiment. He said he was a surgeon, and that in case any accident occurred on board he must always be in readiness. He could not afford to have his nerves unsettled. Perhaps he was quite right, but I am inclined to think that his precaution was prompted by his inclination. On inquiry, he informed me that there was no one on board who would be likely to join me in my investigations, and after a little more conversation I left him. A little later I met the captain, and told him my story. I said that if no one would spend the night with me I would ask leave to have the light burning all night, and would try it alone.

"'Look here,' said he, 'I will tell you what I will do. I will share your watch myself, and we will see what happens. It is my belief that we can find out between us. There may be some fellow skulking on board who steals a passage by frightening the passengers. It is just possible that there may be something queer in the carpentering of that berth.'

"I suggested taking the ship's carpenter below and examining the place; but I was overjoyed at the captain's offer to spend the night with me. He accordingly sent for the workman and ordered him to do anything I required. We went below at once. I had all the bedding cleared out of the upper berth, and we examined the place thoroughly to see if there was a board loose anywhere, or a panel which could be opened or pushed aside. We tried the planks everywhere, tapped the flooring, unscrewed the fittings of the lower berth and took it to pieces—in short, there was not a square inch of the stateroom which was not searched and tested. Everything was in perfect order, and we put everything back in its place. As we were finishing our work, Robert came to the door and looked in.

"'Well, sir—find anything, sir?' he asked with a ghastly grin.

"'You were right about the porthole, Robert,' I said, and I

gave him the promised sovereign.

The carpenter did his work silently and skillfully, following in I could see Robert the steward, who stood a little farther

"'I'm a plain man, sir,' he said. 'But it's my belief you had better just turn out your things and let me run half a dozen four-inch screws through the door of this cabin. There's no good never came o' this cabin yet, sir, and that's all about it. There's been four lives lost out o' here to my own remembrance, and that in four trips. Better give it up, sir—better give it up!'

"'I will try it for one night more,' I said.

"'Better give it up, sir—better give it up! It's a precious bad job,' repeated the workman, putting his tools in his bag and leaving the cabin.

"But my spirits had risen considerably at the prospect of having the captain's company, and I made up my mind not to be prevented from going to the end of the strange business. I abstained from Welsh rarebits that evening, and did not even join in the customary game of whist. I wanted to be quite sure of my nerves, and my vanity made me anxious to make a good figure in the captain's eyes.

IV

"The captain was one of those splendidly tough and cheerful specimens of seafaring humanity whose combined courage, hardihood, and calmness in difficulty leads them naturally into high positions of trust. He was not the man to be led away by an idle tale, and the mere fact that he was willing to join me in the investigation was proof that he thought there was something seriously wrong. To some extent, too, his reputation was at stake, as well as the reputation of the ship. It is no light thing to lose passengers overboard, and he knew it.

"About ten o'clock that evening, as I was smoking a last cigar, he came up to me and drew me aside from the beat of the other passengers who were patrolling the deck in the warm darkness.

" 'This is a serious matter, Mr. Brisbane,' he said. 'We must make up our minds either way—to be disappointed or to have a pretty rough time of it. You see, I cannot afford to laugh at the affair, and I will ask you to sign your name to a statement of whatever occurs. If nothing happens tonight we will try it again tomorrow and next day. Are you ready?'

"So we went below and entered the stateroom. As we went in I could see Robert the steward, who stood a little farther down the passage, watching us, with his usual grin, as though certain that something dreadful was about to happen. The captain closed the door behind us and bolted it.

" 'Supposing we put your portmanteau before the door,' he suggested. 'One of us can sit on it. Nothing can get out then. Is the port screwed down?'

"I found it as I had left it in the morning. Indeed, without using a lever, as I had done, no one could have opened it. I drew back the curtains of the upper berth so that I could see well into it. By the captain's advice I lighted my reading-lantern, and placed it so that it shone upon the white sheets above. He insisted upon sitting on the portmanteau, declaring that he wished to be able to swear that he had sat before the door.

"Then he requested me to search the stateroom thoroughly, an operation very soon accomplished, as it consisted merely in looking beneath the lower berth and under the couch below the porthole. The spaces were quite empty.

" 'It is impossible for any human being to get in,' I said, 'or for any human being to open the port.'

" 'Very good,' said the captain, calmly. 'If we see anything now, it must be either imagination or something supernatural.'

"I sat down on the edge of the lower berth.

"'The first time it happened,' said the captain, crossing his legs and leaning back against the door, 'was in March. The passenger who slept here, in the upper berth, turned out to have been a lunatic—at all events, he was known to have been a little touched, and he had taken his passage without the knowledge of his friends. He rushed out in the middle of the night, and threw himself overboard, before the officer who had the watch could stop him. We stopped and lowered a boat. It was a quiet night, just before that heavy weather came on; but we could not find him. Of course his suicide was afterward accounted for on the ground of his insanity.'

"'I suppose that often happens?' I remarked, rather absently.

"'Not often—no,' said the captain; 'never before in my experience, though I have heard of it happening on board of other ships. Well, as I was saying, that occurred in March. On the very next trip—What are you looking at?' he asked, stopping suddenly in his narration.

"I believe I gave no answer. My eyes were riveted upon the porthole. It seemed to me that the brass loop-nut was beginning to turn very slowly upon the screw—so slowly, however, that I was not sure it moved at all. I watched it intently, fixing its position in my mind, and trying to ascertain whether it changed. Seeing where I was looking, the captain looked too.

"'It moves!' he exclaimed, in a tone of conviction. 'No, it does not,' he added, after a minute.

"'If it were the jarring of the screw,' said I, 'it would have opened during the day; but I found it this evening jammed tight as I left it this morning.'

"I rose and tried the nut. It was certainly loosened, for by an effort I could move it with my hands.

"'The queer thing,' said the captain, 'is that the second

man who was lost is supposed to have got through that very port. We had a terrible time over it. It was in the middle of the night, and the weather was very heavy; there was an alarm that one of the ports was open and the sea running in. I came below and found everything flooded, the water pouring in every time she rolled, and the whole port swinging from the top bolts—not the porthole in the middle. Well, we managed to shut it, but the water did some damage. Ever since then, the place smells of sea water from time to time. We supposed the passenger had thrown himself out, though the Lord only knows how he did it. The steward kept telling me that he could not keep anything shut here. Upon my word—I can smell it now, can't you?' he inquired, sniffing the air suspiciously.

"'Yes—distinctly,' I said, and I shuddered as that same stagnant sea water grew stronger in the cabin. 'Now, to smell like this, the place must be damp,' I continued, 'and yet when I examined it with the carpenter this morning everything was perfectly dry. It is most extraordinary—hallo!'

"My reading-lantern, which had been placed in the upper berth, was suddenly extinguished. There was still a good deal of light from the pane of ground glass near the door, behind which loomed the regulation lamp. The ship rolled heavily, and the curtain of the upper berth swung far out into the stateroom and back again. I rose quickly from my seat on the edge of the bed, and the captain at the same moment started to his feet with a loud cry of surprise. I had turned with the intention of taking down the lantern to examine it, when I heard his exclamation, and immediately afterward his call for help. I sprang toward him. He was wrestling with all his might with the brass loop of the port. It seemed to turn against his hands in spite of all his efforts. I caught up my cane, a heavy oak stick I always used to carry, and thrust it through the ring and bore on it with all my strength. But the strong wood snapped suddenly, and I fell upon the couch.

When I rose again the port was wide open, and the captain was standing with his back against the door, pale to the lips.

"'There is something in that berth!' he cried, in a strange voice, his eyes almost starting from his head. 'Hold the door, while I look—it shall not escape us, whatever it is!'

"But instead of taking his place, I sprang upon the lower bed and seized something which lay in the upper berth.

"It was something ghostly, horrible beyond words, and it moved in my grip. It was like the body of a man long drowned, and yet it moved and had the strength of ten men living; but I gripped it with all my might—the slippery, oozy, horrible thing. The dead white eyes seemed to stare at me out of the dusk; the putrid odor of rank sea water was about it, and its shiny hair hung in foul wet curls over its dead face. I wrestled with the dead thing. It thrust itself upon me and forced me back and nearly broke my arms. It wound its corpse's arms about my neck, the living death, and overpowered me, so that I, at last, cried aloud and fell and let go my hold.

"As I fell, the thing sprang across me and seemed to throw itself upon the captain. When I last saw him on his feet his face was white and his lips set. It seemed to me that he struck a violent blow at the dead being, and then he, too, fell forward upon his face, with an inarticulate cry of horror.

"The thing paused an instant, seeming to hover over his prostrate body, and I could have screamed again for very fright, but I had no voice left. The thing vanished suddenly, and it seemed to my disturbed senses that it made its exit through the open port, though how that was possible, considering the smallness of the aperture, is more than anyone can tell. I lay a long time upon the floor, and the captain lay beside me. At last I partially recovered my senses and moved, and I instantly knew that my arm was broken—the small bone of the left forearm near the wrist.

"I got upon my feet somehow, and with my remaining hand

I tried to raise the captain. He groaned and moved, and at last came to himself. He was not hurt, but he seemed badly stunned.

"Well, do you want to hear any more? There is nothing more. That is the end of my story. The carpenter carried out his scheme of running half a dozen four-inch screws through the door of one hundred and five, and if ever you take a passage in the 'Kamtschatka,' you may ask for a berth in that stateroom. You will be told that it is engaged—yes—it is engaged by that dead thing.

"I finished the trip in the surgeon's cabin. He doctored my broken arm, and advised me not to 'fiddle about with ghosts and things' any more. The captain was very silent, and never sailed again in that ship, though it is still running. And I will not sail in her either. It was a very disagreeable experience and I was very badly frightened, which is a thing I do not like. That is all. That is how I saw a ghost—if it was a ghost. It was dead, anyhow."

The Wonderful Day

Robert Arthur

I

Danny was crouched on the stairs, listening to the grownups talk in the living room below. He wasn't supposed to be there. He was supposed to be in bed, since he was still recovering from the chicken pox.

But it got lonely being in bed all the time, and he hadn't been able to resist slipping out and down in his wool pajamas, to hear Dad and Mom, and Sis and Uncle Ben and Aunt Anna talking.

Dad—he was Dr. Norcross, and everybody went to him when they were sick—and the others were playing bridge. Sis, who was in high school, was studying her Latin, not so hard she couldn't take part in the conversation.

They were mostly talking about other people in Locustville, which was such a small town everybody knew everybody else, well enough to talk about them, anyway.

"Locustville!" That was Mom, with a sigh. "I know it's a pretty town, with the river and the trees and the woods

88

around it, and Tom has a good practice here, but the people! If only something would shake some of them out of themselves, and show them how petty and malicious and miserable they are!"

"Like Nettie Peters," Dad said, his tone dry. Danny knew Miss Peters. Always hurrying over to some neighbor's to talk about somebody. Whisper-whisper-whisper. Saying nasty things. "She's the source of most of the gossip in this town. If ever there was a woman whose tongue was hinged in the middle and wagged at both ends, it's her."

Uncle Ben laughed.

"Things would be better here," he remarked, "if the money were better distributed. If Jacob Earl didn't own or have a mortgage on half the town, there might be more free thought and tolerance. But nobody in debt to him dares open his mouth."

"Funny thing," Dad put in, "how some men have a knack of making money at other men's expense. Everything Jacob Earl touches seems to mint money for him—money that comes out of someone else's pocket. Like the gravel land he got from John Wiggins. I'd like to see the process reversed sometime."

"But for real miserliness"—that was Aunt Anna, indignant —"Luke Hawks takes all the prizes. I've seen him come into the Fair-Square store to buy things for his children, and the trouble he had letting go his money, you'd have thought it stuck to his fingers!"

"It's a question," Dad said, "which is worse, miserliness or shiftlessness. Miserliness, I suppose, because most shiftless people are at least good-hearted. Like Henry Jones. Henry wishes for more things and does less to get them than any man in Christendom. If wishes were horses, Henry would have the biggest herd this side of the Mississippi."

"Well, there are some nice people in Locustville," Sis broke into the conversation. "I don't care what that old gossip Miss

Peters says, or that stuck-up Mrs. Norton either; I think Miss Avery, my English and gym teacher, is swell. She isn't awful pretty, but she's nice.

"There's little silver bells in her voice when she talks, and if that Bill Morrow whose dad owns the implement factory, and who takes time off to coach the football team wasn't a dope, he'd have fallen for her long ago. She's crazy about him, but too proud to show it, and that silly Betty Norton has made him think he's wonderful by playing up to him all the time."

"If he marries Betty," Aunt Anna said, "the town won't be able to hold Mrs. Norton any more. She's already so puffed up with being the wife of the bank president and the leader of the town's social life, she'd just swell up a little more and float away like a balloon if she got the Morrow Implement Company for a son-in-law."

Everybody laughed, and the conversation slowly died away.

Mom mentioned how much she disliked the two-faced Minerva Benson who was so nice to people's faces and worked against them behind their backs.

Sis said that Mr. Wiggins, who ran the bookstore, was a nice little man who ought to marry Miss Wilson, the dressmaker, a plain little woman who would be as pretty as a picture if she *looked* the way she *was*.

But he never would, Sis said, because he hadn't any money and would be ashamed to ask a woman to marry him when he couldn't even earn his own living.

Then they went back to bridge. Danny was feeling sort of weak and shaky, so he hurried back to bed before Mom could catch him. He crawled in and pulled the blankets up over him, and then his hand reached under the pillow and pulled out the funny thing he'd found in the old chest where he kept his games and skates and things.

It had been wrapped in a soft piece of leather, and he had

found it in a little space behind one of the drawers. There was a name inked on the leather, *Jonas Norcross.* Dad's grandfather had been named Jonas, so it might have been originally his.

What the thing was was a little pointed piece of ivory, sharp at the tip and round at the bottom, as if it had been sawed off the very end of an elephant's tusk.

Only there was a fine spiral line in it, like in a snail's shell, that made Danny think maybe it hadn't come from an elephant, but from an animal he had seen in a book once— an animal like a horse, with one long horn over its nose. He couldn't remember the name.

It was all yellow with age, and on the bottom was carved a funny mark, all cross lines, very intricate. Maybe it was Chinese writing. Jonas Norcross had been captain of a clipper ship in the China trade, so it might have come all the way from China.

Lying in bed, Danny held the bit of ivory in his hand. It gave out a warmth to his fingers that was nice. Holding it tight, he thought of a picture in his book about King Arthur's Round Table—a picture of Queen Guinevere of the golden hair. Probably it was a picture like that Sis had meant Miss Wilson ought to be pretty as.

Grownups' talk wasn't always easy to understand, the way they said things that weren't so.

Danny yawned. Gee, though, it would be awful funny— He yawned again, and the weight of drowsiness descending on him closed his eyes. But not before one last thought had floated through his mind.

As it came to him, a queer little breeze seemed to spring up in the room. It fluttered the curtains and rattled the window shade. For just a second Danny felt almost as if somebody was in the room with him. Then it was gone, and smiling at his amusing thought, Danny slept.

II

Henry Jones woke that morning with the smell of frying bacon in his nostrils. He yawned and stretched, comfortably. There was a clock on the bureau the other side of the room, but it was too much trouble to look at it.

He looked at where the sunshine, coming in the window, touched the carpet. That told him it was just onto nine.

Downstairs pans were rattling. Martha was up and about, long ago. And just about ready to get impatient with him for lingering in bed.

"Ho *huuuum!*" Henry yawned, and pushed down the covers. "I wish I was up an' dressed aw-ready."

As if it were an echo to his yawn, a shrill whickering sound reached him from the direction of his large, untidy backyard. Disregarding it, Henry slid into his trousers and shirt, his socks and shoes, put on a tie, combed his hair casually, and ambled down to the dining room.

"Well!" his wife, Martha, commented tartly, appearing in the doorway with a platter in her hands as he slumped down into his chair. "It's after nine. If you're going to look for work today, you should have been started long ago!"

Henry shook his head dubiously as she set the bacon and eggs in front of him.

"I dunno if I ought to go tramping around today," he muttered. "Don't feel so well. Mmm, that looks good. But I kind of wish we could have sausage oncet in a while."

From the rear yard came another high whinny that went unnoticed.

"Sausage is expensive," Martha told him. "When you get an honest job, maybe we can afford some."

"There's Hawks," Henry remarked, with interest, peering out the front window as a lean, long-faced man strode past the house, with a pleasant but shabbily-dressed little woman trotting meekly at his side. "Guess Millie has talked him into laying out some money for new things for the kids at last. It's only about once a year she gets him to loosen up."

"And then you'd think, to look at him, he was dying," his wife commented, "just because he's buying a couple of pairs of two-dollar shoes for two as nice youngsters as ever lived. He begrudges them every mouthful they eat, almost."

"Still," Henry said, wagging his head wisely, "I wish I had the money he has stacked away."

From the rear yard came a sound of galloping hooves. Martha was too intent on scolding Henry to notice it.

"Wish, wish, wish!" she stormed. "But never work, work, work! Oh, Henry, you're the most exasperating man alive!"

"Martha, I'm not worthy of you," Henry sighed. "I wish you had a better husband. I mean it."

This time the whinnying behind the house was a concerted squeal from many throats, too loud to go unnoticed. Henry's buxom wife started, looked puzzled, and hurried out to the kitchen. A moment later her screech reached Henry's ears.

"Henry! The back yard's full of horses! Plunging and kicking all over the place!"

The news was startling enough to overcome Henry's early-morning lethargy. He joined his wife at the kitchen window and stared with popping eyes at the big rear yard.

It was full—anyway, it seemed full—of animals. Martha had called them horses. They weren't exactly horses. But they weren't ponies either. They were too small to be the one and too big to be the other. And they were covered with longish hair, had wild flowing manes, and looked strong and savage enough to lick their weight in tigers.

"Well, I'll be deuced!" Henry exclaimed, his round countenance vastly perplexed. "I wish I knew where those critters came from."

"Henry!" Martha wailed, clutching his arm. "Now there's five!"

There had been four of them, trotting about the yard, nosing at the wreck of the car Henry had once driven, thumping with their hooves the board fence that penned them in. But now there were, indeed, five.

"G-gosh!" Henry gulped, his Adam's apple working up and down. "We must have counted wrong. Now, how do you suppose they got in there?"

"But what kind of horses are they, Henry?" Martha asked, holding to his arm still, as if for protection, in a way she hadn't for years. "And whom do you suppose they belong to?"

Henry put an arm around Martha's plump waist and applied a reassuring pressure.

"I wish I knew, Martha," he muttered. "I wish I knew."

"Henry!" There was real fright in his wife's voice. "Now there's six!"

"Seven," Henry corrected weakly. "The other two just— just sort of appeared."

Together they gazed at the seven shaggy ponies that were trotting restlessly about the yard, nosing at the fence as if seeking escape from the limited space.

No more appeared; and seeing the number remain staple, Henry and Martha gained more self-possession.

"Henry," his wife said with severity, as if somehow blaming him, "there's something queer happening. Nobody ever saw horses like those in Indiana before."

"Maybe they belong to a circus." Henry suggested, staring in fascination at the seven uncouth beasts.

"Maybe they belong to us!"

"Us?" Henry's jaw dropped. "How could they belong to us?"

"Henry," his wife told him, "you've got to go out and see

if they're branded. I remember reading anybody can claim a wild horse if it hasn't been branded. And those are wild horses if I ever saw any."

Of course, Martha never *had* seen any wild horses, but her words sounded logical. Her husband, however, made no motion toward the back door.

"Listen," he said, "Martha, you stay here and watch. Don't let anybody into the yard. I'm going to get Jake Harrison, at the stable. He used to be a horse trader. He'll know what those things are and if they belong to us, if anybody does."

"All right, Henry," his wife agreed—the first time he could remember her agreeing with him in, anyway, two years—"but hurry. Please do hurry."

"I will!" Henry vowed; and without even snatching up his hat, he shot away.

Jake Harrison, the livery stable owner, came back with him unwillingly, half dragged in Henry's excitement. But when he stood in the kitchen and stared out at the yard full of horses, his incredulity vanished.

"Good Lord!" he gasped. "Henry, where'd you get 'em?"

"Never mind that," Henry told him. "Just tell me, what *are* they?"

"Mongolian ponies," the lanky horse dealer informed him. "The exact kind of ponies old Ghengis Khan's men rode on when they conquered most of the known world. I've seen pictures of them in books. Imagine it! Mongolian ponies here in Locustville!"

"Well," Martha asked, with withering scorn, "aren't you going out to see if they're branded? Or are you two men afraid of a lot of little ponies?"

"I guess they won't hurt us," the stable owner decided, "if we're careful. Come on, Henry, let's see if I'm still any good at lassoing. Mis' Jones, can I use this hank of clothesline?"

Henry opened the kitchen door and followed Jake Harrison

out into the yard. At their advent the seven ponies—he was glad to see the number hadn't changed in his absence— stopped their restless trotting and lifted their heads to stare at the men.

Jake made a noose out of the clothesline and began to circle it above his head. The ponies snorted and reared, suspiciously. Picking the smallest one, the tall man let the noose go, and it settled over the creature's thick neck.

The pony's nostrils flared. It reared and beat the air with its unshod front hooves as the other six broke and scampered to the opposite end of the yard.

Jake Harrison drew the loop tight and approached the pony, making soothing sounds. It quieted and, as the two men came close, let Jake put his hands on it.

"Yes, sir," the stable owner exclaimed, "a real honest-to-Homer Mongolian pony. That long hair is to keep the cold out, up in the mountains of Tibet. Now let's see if there's any brand. None on its hide. Let's see its hoof."

The pony let him lift its left forefoot without protest, and Henry, bending close, let out a whoop.

"Look, Jake!" he yelled. "It's branded! With my name! These critters are mine!"

Together they stared. Cut into the hard horn, in neat letters, was HENRY JONES.

Jake straightened.

"Yours, all right," he agreed. "Now, Henry, stop making a mystery and tell me where these animals came from."

Henry's jubilance faded. He shook his head.

"Honest, Jake, I don't know. I wish I did. . . . *Look out!*"

The tall man leaped back. Between them an eighth pony had appeared, so close that its flanks brushed against them.

"W-where—" Jake stuttered, backing away toward the door in the fence and fumbling for the catch. "Where—"

"That's what I don't know!" Henry joined him. "That's what I wish—No, I don't either! I don't wish anything at all!"

The phantom pony that had appeared directly before them, wispy and tenuous as darkish smoke, promptly vanished.

Henry mopped his face.

"Did you see what I saw?" he asked; and Jake, swallowing hard, nodded.

"You st-started to wish for something, and it st-started to appear," he gobbled, and thrust open the door in the board fence. "Let's get out o' here."

"When I started to wish—Oh, jiminy crickets!" Henry groaned. "That's how the others happened. When I wished. Do you suppose—Do you—"

Pale-faced, they stared at each other. Slowly the stableman nodded.

"Lord!" the ashen Henry whispered. "I never believed such a thing could happen. I wish now I'd never—"

This time the words weren't fully out of his mouth before the ninth pony struck the earth with a sudden plop directly before them.

It was too much. Henry broke and ran, and Jake followed at his heels. The pony, interestedly, chased them. Its brothers, not to be left behind, streamed through the opening in the fence, whickering gleefully.

When Henry and Jake brought up, around the corner of the house, they were just in time to look back and see the last of the beasts trotting out into Main Street. Nine wicked whinnies cut through the morning quiet. Nine sets of small hooves pounded.

"They're stampeding!" Henry shrilled. "Jake, we got to round 'em up before they do lots of damage. Oh, Jehosephat, I wish this hadn't ever happened!"

Neighing raucously, the tenth pony kicked up its heels, throwing dirt in their faces, and set off at a gallop after the others.

III

About the time Henry Jones was running for Jake Harrison, Luke Hawks was fingering a boy's woolen suit with lean, predatory digits.

"This be the cheapest?" he asked, and being assured that it was—all the clerks in Locustville knew better than to show him anything but the least expensive—nodded.

"I'll take it," he said, and grudgingly reached for his hip pocket.

"Don't you think the material is kind of thin, Luke?" little Emily Hawks asked, a note of pleading in her voice. "Last winter Billy had colds all the time, and Ned—"

The man did not bother to answer. With the well-filled wallet in his left hand, he inserted thumb and forefinger and brought out a twenty-dollar bill.

"Here," he said. "And I've got thirteen dollars forty cents coming."

Taking the bill and starting to turn away, the clerk turned abruptly back. Luke Hawks had snatched the money from his hand.

"Is anything—" he began, and stopped. Testily the man was still holding out the note.

"Take it," he snapped. "Don't make me stand here waiting."

"Yes, sir." The clerk apologized, and took a firmer hold. But he could not take the bill from Luke Hawks. He pulled. Hawks' hand jerked forward. Scowling, the lean man drew his hand back. The money came with it.

"What's the matter, Luke?" Emily Hawks asked. Her husband favored her with a frown.

"Some glue on it, or something," he muttered. "It stuck to my fingers. I'll get another bill out, young man."

He put the twenty back into the wallet—where it went easily enough—and drew out two tens. But neither would these leave his hand.

Luke Hawks was beginning to go a little pale. He trans-
ferred the notes to his left hand. But though his left hand
could take them from his right, the clerk could take them
from neither. Whenever he tugged at it, the money simply
would not come loose. It stuck as close to Luke Hawks'
fingers as if it were part of his skin.

A red flush crept into the man's cheeks. He could not
meet his wife's gaze.

"I—I dunno—" he muttered. "I'll lay it down. You pick it
up."

Carefully he laid a ten-dollar bill on the counter, spread
his fingers wide, and lifted his hand. To his horror and fright,
the bit of green paper came with it, adhering firmly to his
fingertips.

"Luke Hawks," his wife said sturdily, "it's a judgment on
you. The good Lord has put a curse on your money."

"Hush!" Hawks warned. "Netty Peters has come in the
store and is looking. She'll hear you and go gabbing nonsense
all—"

"It is not nonsense!" his wife stated. "It's truth. Your
money will not leave your fingers."

Luke Hawks went deathly pale again. With a strangled
curse, he snatched out all the money in his wallet and tried
to throw it down on the counter. To his intense relief, one
folded green slip fluttered down, though the rest remained in
his hand.

"There!" he gasped. "It ain't so! Boy, how much is that?"
The clerk reached for the paper.

"It—it's a cigar coupon, sir," he reported, his face wooden.

Luke Hawks wilted then. He thrust all his money into the
ancient pigskin wallet and being careful his fingers touched
only the leather, held it out to his wife.

"Here!" he directed. "You pay him, Emily."

Emily Hawks folded her arms and looked straight into his
frightened eyes.

"Luke Hawks," she said, in a firm, clear voice that carried through the entire store, "for eight years my life has been made a misery by your mean, grasping ways. Now you can't spend any of your money. You'll starve to death before you can even spend a nickel for bread.

"And I've a good mind to let you. If I don't buy anything for you, you can be sure no one will give it to you. The people of this town would laugh themselves sick seeing you with your hands full of money, begging for a bite to eat. They wouldn't give it to you, either."

Luke Hawks knew they wouldn't. He stared down at his wife, who had never before dared act like this.

"No," he protested. "Emily, don't say that. Here, you take the money. Spend it as you want. Get the things we need. I'll leave it all to you. You—you can even get the next most expensive clothes for the boys."

"You mean you want me to handle the money from now on?" Emily Hawks demanded, and her husband nodded.

"Yes, Emily," he gasped. "Take it. Please take it."

His wife took the wallet—which left Luke Hawks' hands readily enough—and counted the money in it.

"Five hundred dollars," she said aloud, thoughtfully. "Luke, hadn't you better give me a check for what you've got in the bank? If I'm to do all the buying, the money'll have to be in my hands."

"A check!" Luke exclaimed. "That's it! I don't need money! I'll pay by check."

"Try it," Emily invited. "That's the same as cash, isn't it?"

Luke tried it. The check would not leave his fingers either. It only tore to pieces when the clerk tugged at it.

After that, he capitulated. He took out his book and signed a blank check, which Emily was able to take. She then filled it in for herself for the entire balance in the bank—twenty thousand dollars, Luke Hawks admitted with strangled reluctance.

After that she tucked the check into the bosom of her dress.

"Now, Luke," she suggested, "you might as well go on home. I'll go to the bank and deposit this to my account. Then I'll do the rest of the shopping. I won't need you."

"But how'll you get the things home?" her husband asked weakly.

Emily Hawks was already almost to the door—out which Netty Peters had just dashed to spread the news through the town. But she paused long enough to turn and smile brightly at her pale and perspiring husband.

"I'll have the man at the garage drive me out with them," she answered. "In the car I'm going to buy after I leave the bank, Luke."

IV

Miss Wilson looked up from her sewing at the sound of galloping hooves in the street outside her tiny shop.

She was just in time to see a small swift figure race by. Then, before she could wonder what it was, she caught sight of herself in the big mirror customers used when trying on the dresses she made.

Her whole name was Alice Wilson. But it was years since anyone had called her by her first name. She was thirty-three, as small and plain as a church mouse—

But she wasn't! Miss Wilson stared open-mouthed at her reflection. She—she wasn't mouse-like any longer. She was— yes, really—almost pretty!

A length of dress goods forgotten in one hand, a needle suspended in mid-air in the other, Alice Wilson stared at the woman in the glass. A small woman, with a smiling, pink and white face, over which a stray lock of golden hair had fallen from the piled-up mass of curls on the top of her head—curls that gave out a soft and shining light.

The woman in the mirror had soft, warm red lips and blue eyes of sky-azure clearness and depth. Alice Wilson stared, and smiled in sheer delight. The image smiled back.

Wonderingly, Alice touched her face with her fingers. What had happened? What kind of a trick were her eyes playing on her? How—

The clatter of hurrying footsteps made her jump. Netty Peters, her sharp face alight with excitement, her head thrust forward on her skinny neck like a running chicken's, ran in. Miss Wilson's dressmaking shop, the closest place to the Fair-Square store, was her first stop on her tour to spread the news of Luke Hawks' curse.

"Miss Wilson," she gobbled breathlessly, "what do you think—"

"*She thinks you've come to spread some scandal or other, that's what she thinks,*" a shrill, file-like voice interrupted.

The voice seemed to come from her own mouth. Netty Peters glared.

"Miss Wilson," she snapped, "if you think ventriloquism is funny when I'm trying to tell you—*just like you're going to tell everybody else!*" the second voice broke in, and Netty Peters felt faint. The words *had* come from her own mouth!

She put her hands to her throat; and because her mind was blank with fright, her tongue went busily ahead with what she had planned to say.

"I saw Luke Hawks—*just like you see everything*"—that was the shrill, second voice, alternating with her own normal one —"in the Fair-Square store and they—*were minding their own business, something you might do*—they were buying clothes for their poor starved children whom they treat so shamefully— *trust you to get that in!*—when Mr. Hawks tried to pay the clerk—*and you were watching to see how much they spent*—the money wouldn't leave his fingers—*did you ever think how many people would be happy if sometimes the words wouldn't leave your throat?*"

The town gossip ceased. Her words had become all jumbled together, making no sense, like two voices trying to shout each other down. There was a strange fluttering in her throat. As if she were talking with two tongues at the same time. . . .

Miss Wilson was staring at her strangely, and Netty Peters saw for the first time the odd radiance in Miss Wilson's hair, the new sweetness in her features.

Incoherent words gurgled in the older woman's throat. Terror glazed her eyes. She turned, and with a queer sobbing wail, fled.

Alice Wilson was still looking after her in bewilderment when another figure momentarily darkened the doorway. It was Mr. Wiggins, who owned the unprofitable bookstore on the other side of her dressmaking establishment.

Ordinarily Mr. Wiggins was a shy, pale-faced man, his thirty-eight years showing in the stoop of his shoulders, his eyes squinting behind thick glasses. He often smiled, but it was the small, hopeful smile of a man who didn't dare not to smile for fear he might lose heart altogether.

But today, this day of strange happenings, Mr. Wiggins was standing erect. His hair was rumpled, his glasses were awry, and his eyes blazed with excitement.

"Miss Wilson!" he cried. "The most amazing thing has happened! I had to tell somebody. I hope you don't mind my bursting in to tell you."

Alice Wilson stared at him, and instantly forgot about the strange thing that had happened to her.

"Oh, *no!*" she answered. "Of course I don't. I—I'm glad!"

Outside there were more sounds of galloping hooves, shrill squeals, and men's voices shouting.

"There seems to be a herd of wild ponies loose in the

town," Mr. Wiggins told Miss Wilson. "One almost knocked me down, racing along the sidewalk as I was coming here. Miss Wilson, you'll never believe it, what I was going to tell you. You'll have to see for yourself. Then you won't think I'm mad."

"Oh, I'd never think that!" Miss Wilson assured him.

Scarcely hearing her, Mr. Wiggins seized her by the hand and almost dragged her to the door. A flush of warm pleasure rose into Miss Wilson's cheeks at the touch of his hand.

A little breathless, she ran beside him, out the shop door, down a dozen yards, and into the gloom of his tiny, unpatronized bookstore.

On the way, she barely had a glimpse of three or four shaggy ponies snorting and wheeling farther up the street, with Henry Jones and Jake Harrison, assisted by a crowd of laughing men and boys, trying to catch them.

Then Mr. Wiggins, trembling with excitement, was pushing her down into an old overstuffed chair.

"Miss Wilson," he said tensely, "I was sitting right here when in came Jacob Earl, not fifteen minutes ago. You know how he walks—big and pompous, as if he owned the earth. I knew what he wanted. He wanted the thousand dollars I owe him, that I borrowed to buy my stock of books with. And I—I didn't have it. None of it.

"You remember when my aunt died last year, she left me that property down by the river that I sold to Jacob Earl for five hundred dollars? He pretended he was just doing me a favor buying it, to help me get started in business.

"But then high-grade gravel was discovered on the land, and now it's worth at least fifteen thousand dollars. I learned Earl knew about the gravel all the time. But in spite of that, he wanted the thousand he loaned me."

"Yes, oh yes!" Miss Wilson exclaimed. "He would. But what did you *do,* Mr. Wiggins?"

Mr. Wiggins combed back his disheveled hair with his fingers.

"I told him I didn't have it. And he took off his glove—his right glove—and told me if I didn't have it by tomorrow, he'd have to attach all my books and fixtures. And then he put his hand down on top of my little brass Chinese luck piece. And guess what happened!"

"Oh, I couldn't!" Miss Wilson whispered. "I never could!"

"Look!" Mr. Wiggins' voice trembled. He snatched up a large dust cloth that hid something on the counter just in front of Miss Wilson's eyes. Underneath the cloth was a squat little Chinese god, about a foot high, sitting with knees crossed and holding a bowl in his lap.

On his brass countenance was a sly smile, and his mouth was open in a round O of great amusement.

And as Miss Wilson stared at him, a small gold coin popped out of the little god's mouth and landed with a musical chink in the bowl in his lap!

Alice Wilson gasped. "Oh, John!" she cried, using Mr. Wiggins' Christian name for the first time in her life. "Is it—is it money?"

"Chinese money," Mr. Wiggins told her. "And the bowl is full of it. A gold coin comes out of his mouth every second. The first one came out right after Mr. Earl put his hand on the god's head. Look!"

He scooped up the contents of the bowl and held them out, let them rain into Miss Wilson's lap. Incredulously she picked one up.

It was a coin as large perhaps as an American nickel. In the center was punched a square hole. All around the edges were queer Oriental ideographs. And the piece of money was as fresh and new and shiny as if it had just come from the mint.

"Is it real gold?" she asked tremulously.

"Twenty carats pure at least!" John Wiggins assured her. "Even if it is Chinese money, the coins must be worth five dollars apiece just for the metal. And look—the bowl is half full again."

They stared wide-eyed and breathless at the little grinning god. Every second, as regularly as clockwork, another gold coin popped out of his open mouth.

"It's as if—as if he were coining them!" John Wiggins whispered.

"Oh, it's wonderful!" Alice Wilson told him, with rapture. "John, I'm so glad! For your sake. Now you can pay off Earl."

"In his own coin!" the man chortled. "Because he started it happening, you know, so you could call it his own coin. Perhaps he pressed a secret spring or something that released them from where they were hidden inside the god. I don't know.

"But the funny thing is, he couldn't pick them up! He tried to pretend he had just dropped the first couple, but they rolled out of the bowl and right across the floor when he reached for them. And then he began to get frightened. He grabbed up his hat and his gloves and ran out."

Then John Wiggins paused. He was looking down at Alice Wilson, and for the first time he really saw the change that had occurred in her.

"Why—why—" he said, "do you know, your hair is the same color as the coins?"

"Oh, it isn't!" Miss Wilson protested, blushing scarlet at the first compliment a man had paid her in ten years.

"It is," he insisted. "And you—you're lovely, Alice. I never realized before how lovely. You're as pretty as—as pretty as a picture!"

He looked down into her eyes, and without taking his gaze away, reached down and took her hands in his. He drew her up out of the chair, and still crimsoning with pleasure, Alice Wilson stood and faced him.

"Alice," John Wiggins said, "Alice, I've known you for a long time, and I've been blind. I guess worry blinded me. Or

I'd have seen long ago how beautiful you are and known what I've just realized. I know I'm not much of a success as a man but—but Alice, would you be my wife?"

Alice Wilson gave a little sigh and rested her face against his shoulder so that he might not see the tears in her eyes. Happiness had mostly eluded her until now, but this moment more than made up for all the years that were past.

John Wiggins put his arms about her, and behind them the little god grinned and went busily on with his minting. . . .

Jacob Earl stamped into his library in his home and locked the door behind him, with fingers that shook a little.

Throwing his hat and stick down, with his gloves, onto a chair, he groped for a cigar in his desk and lit it, by sheer force of will striving to quell the inward agitation that was shaking him.

But—Well, any man might feel shaken if he had put his hand down on a cold brass paperweight and had felt the thing twist in his grip as if alive, had felt a shock in his fingers like a sudden discharge of electricity, and then had seen the thing start to spout gold money.

Money—and Jacob Earl gazed down at his soft, plump white hands almost with fright—which had *life* in it. Because when he had tried to pick it up, it had eluded him. It had *dodged.*

Angrily he flung away his barely smoked cigar. Hallucinations! He'd been having a dizzy spell, or—or something. Or Wiggins had fixed up a trick to play on him. That was it, a trick!

The nerve of the man, giving him such a start! When he had finished with the little rabbit he—he—

Jacob Earl did not quite formulate what he would do. But the mere thought of threatening somebody made him feel better. He'd decide later what retaliation he would make.

Right now, he'd get to work. He'd inventory his strong box.

Nothing like handling hard, tangible possessions, like stocks and bonds and gold, to restore a man's nerves when he felt shaky.

He spun the combination of his safe, swung open the heavy outer door, unlocked the inner door, and slid out first a weighty steel cash box locked by a massive padlock.

Weighty, because it held the one thing a man couldn't have too much of—gold. Pure gold ingots, worth five hundred dollars each. Fifteen thousand dollars' worth of them.

He'd had them since long before the government called in gold. And he was going to keep them, government or no. If he ever had to sell them, he'd claim they'd been forgotten, and found again by accident.

Jacob Earl flung open the lid of his gold cache. And his overly ruddy face turned a sudden pallid gray. Two of the ingots in the top layer were missing!

But no one could get into his safe. No one but himself. It wasn't possible that a thief—

Then the gray of his face turned to ashen white. He stared, his breath caught in his throat. As he stared, a third ingot had vanished. Evaporated. Into thin air. As if an unseen hand had closed over it and snatched it away.

But it wasn't possible! Such a thing couldn't happen.

And then the fourth ingot vanished. Transfixed by rage and fright, he put his hands down on the remaining yellow bars and pressed with all his might.

But presently the fifth of his precious chunks of metal slipped away from beneath his very fingers into nothingness. One instant it was there, and he could feel it. Then—gone!

With a hoarse cry, Jacob Earl dropped the cash box. He stumbled across the room to his telephone, got a number.

"Doctor?" he gasped. "Doctor Norcross? This is Jacob Earl. I—I—"

Then he bethought himself. This couldn't happen. This was madness. If he told anyone—

"Never mind, doctor!" he blurted. "Sorry to have troubled you. It's all right."

He hung up. And sat there, all the rest of the day, sweat beading his brow, watching the shiny yellow oblongs that had fallen on the floor vanish one by one.

In another part of town, another hand crept toward the telephone—and drew back. Minerva Benson's hand. Minerva Benson had discovered her deformity almost the instant she had arisen, late that morning. The stiff, lifeless face affixed to the back of her head now. Thin, vicious, twisted, the features of a harpy.

With trembling fingers she touched it again, in a wild hope that it might have vanished. Then she huddled closer on the end of the sofa in the darkened room, whose door was locked, blinds drawn.

She couldn't telephone. Because no one must see her like this. No one. Not even a doctor. . . .

And in her tiny, spinsterish home Netty Peters also crouched, and also feared to telephone.

Feared, lest that strange, dreadful second voice begin to clack and rattle in her throat when she tried to talk, tried to ask Doctor Norcross to come.

Crouched, and felt her throat with fingers like frantic claws. And was sure she could detect something moving in her throat like a thing alive.

V

Mrs. Edward Norton moved along the tree-shaded streets toward the downtown section of Locustville with all the self-conscious pride of a frigate entering a harbor under full sail.

She was a full-bodied woman—well built, she phrased it—
and expensively dressed. Certainly the best-dressed woman in
town, as befitted her position as leader of Locustville's social
life and the most influential woman in town.

And today she was going to use her influence. She was
going to have Janice Avery discharged as teacher in the high
school.

Distinctly she had seen the young woman *smoking* in her
room, the previous evening, as she happened to be driving by.
A woman who should be an example to the children she
taught actually—

Mrs. Norton sailed along, indignation high in her. She had
called first at Minerva Benson's home. Minerva was a member of the school board. But Minerva had said she was sick,
and refused to see her.

Then she had tried Jacob Earl, the second member of the
board. And he had been ill too.

It was odd.

Now she was going directly to the office of Doctor Norcross. He was head of the school board. Not the kind of man
she approved of for the position, of course—

Mrs. Norton paused. For the past few moments she had
been experiencing a strange sensation of puffiness, of lightness.
Was she ill too? Could she be feeling light-headed or dizzy?

But no, she was perfectly normal. Just a moment's upset
perhaps, from walking too fast.

She continued onward. What had she been thinking? Oh,
yes, Doctor Norcross. An able physician, perhaps, but his
wife was really quite—well, quite a dowdy. . . .

Mrs. Norton paused again. A gentle breeze was blowing
down the street and she—she was being swayed from side to
side by it. Actually, it was almost pushing her off balance!

She took hold of a convenient lamppost. That stopped her
from swaying. But—

She stared transfixed at her fingers. They were swollen and puffy.

Her rings were cutting into them painfully. Could she have some awful—

Then she became aware of a strained, uncomfortable feeling all over her person. A feeling of being confined, intolerably pent-up in her clothing.

With her free hand she began to pat herself, at first with puzzlement, then with terror. Her clothing was as tight on her as the skin of a sausage. It had shrunk! It was cutting off her circulation!

No, it hadn't. That wasn't true. She was growing! Puffing up! Filling out her clothes like a slowly expanding balloon.

Her corset was confining her diaphragm, making it impossible to breathe. She couldn't get air into her lungs.

She had some awful disease. That was what came of living in a dreadful, dirty place like Locustville, among backward, ignorant people who carried germs and—

At that instant the laces of Mrs. Norton's corsets gave way. She could actually feel herself swell, bloat, puff out. Her arms were queer and hard to handle. The seams of her dress were giving way.

The playful breeze pushed her, and she swayed back and forth like a midnight drunk staggering homeward.

Her fingers slipped from the lamppost.

And she began to rise slowly, ponderously into the air, like a runaway balloon.

Mrs. Edward Norton screamed. Piercingly. But her voice seemed lost, a thin wail that carried hardly twenty yards. This was unthinkable. This was impossible!

But it was happening.

Now she was a dozen feet above the sidewalk. Now twenty. And at that level she paused, spinning slowly around and around, her arms flopping like a frightened chicken's wings, her mouth opening and closing like a feeding goldfish's, but no sounds coming forth.

If anyone should see her now! Oh, if anyone should see her!

But no one did. The street was quite deserted. The houses were few, and set well back from the street. And the excitement downtown, the herd of strange ponies that all day had been kicking up their heels, as Henry Jones and his volunteer assistants tried to pen them up, had drawn every unoccupied soul in Locustville.

Mrs. Norton, pushed along by the gentle breeze, began to drift slowly northward toward the town limits.

Tree branches scraped her and ripped her stockings as she clutched unavailingly at them. A crow, attracted by the strange spectacle, circled around her several times, emitted a raucous squawk that might have been amusement, and flew off.

A stray dog, scratching fleas in the sunshine, saw her pass overhead and followed along underneath for a moment, barking furiously.

Mrs. Norton crimsoned with shame and mortification. Oh, if anyone saw her!

But if no one saw her, no one could help her. She did not know whether to pray for someone to come along or not. She was unhurt. Perhaps nothing worse was going to happen.

But to be sailing placidly through the air, twenty feet above the street, puffed up like a balloon!

The breeze had brought her out to a district marked for subdivision, but still vacant. Fruit trees grew upon the land. The playful wind, shifting its quarter, altered her course. In a moment she was drifting past the upper branches of gnarled old apple trees, quite hidden from the street.

Her clothes were torn, her legs and arms scratched, her hair was straggling down her back. And her indignation and fear of being seen began to give way to a sensation of awful helplessness. She, the most important woman in Locustville, to be blowing around among a lot of old fruit trees for crows to caw at and dogs to bark at and—

Mrs. Norton gasped. She had just risen another three feet. With that she began to weep.

The tears streamed down her face. All at once she felt humble and helpless and without a thought for her dignity or her position. She just wanted to get down.

She just wanted to go home and have Edward pat her shoulder and say, "There, there," as he used to—a long time ago—while she had a good cry on his shoulder.

She was a bad woman, and being punished for it. She had been puffed up with pride, and this was what came of it. In the future, if ever she got down safely, she'd know better.

As if influenced by the remorseful thoughts, she began to descend slowly. Before she was aware of it, she had settled into the upper branches of a cherry tree, scaring away a flock of indignant robins.

And there she caught.

She had quite a lot of time in which to reflect before she saw Janice Avery swinging past along a short cut from the school to her home, and called to her.

Janice Avery got her down. With the aid of Bill Morrow, who was the first person she could find when she ran back to the school to get aid.

Bill was just getting into his car to drive out to the football field, where he was putting the school team through spring practice, when she ran up; and at first he did not seem to understand what she was saying.

As a matter of fact, he didn't. He was just hearing her voice—a voice that was cool and sweet and lovely, like music against a background of distant silver bells.

Then, when he got it, he sprang into action.

"Good Lord!" he exclaimed. "Mrs. Norton stuck up a tree picking cherries? I can't believe it."

But he got a ladder from the school and brought it, gulping at the sight of the stout, tearful woman caught in the crotch of the cherry tree.

A few moments later they had her down. Mrs. Norton made no effort to explain beyond the simple statement she had first made to Janice.

"I was picking cherries and I just got stuck."

Wild as it was, it was better than the truth.

Bill Morrow brought his car as close as he could and Janice hurried her out to it, torn, scratched, bedraggled, red-eyed. They got her in without anyone seeing and drove her home.

Mrs. Norton sobbed out a choked thanks and fled into the house, to weep on the shoulders of her surprised husband.

Bill Morrow mopped his forehead and looked at Janice Avery. She wasn't pretty, but—Well, there was something in her face. Something swell. And her voice. A man could hear a voice like that all his life and not grow tried of it.

"Lord!" he exclaimed, as he slid behind the wheel of his car. "And Betty Norton is going to look just like that some day. Whew! Do you know, I'm a fool. I actually once thought of—But never mind. Where can I take you?"

He grinned at her, and Janice Avery smiled back, little happy lines springing into life around the corners of her lips and her eyes.

"Well," she began, as the wide-shouldered young man kicked the motor into life, "you have to get to practice—"

"Practice is out!" Bill Morrow told her with great firmness, and let in the clutch. "We're going some place and talk!"

She sat back, content.

VI

The sun was setting redly as Dr. Norcross closed his office and swung off homeward with a lithe step.

It had been a strange day. Very strange. Wild ponies had been running through the town since morning, madly chased by the usually somnolent Henry Jones. From his window he had seen into the bookstore across the street and distinctly perceived John Wiggins and Alice Wilson embracing.

Then there had been that abortive phone call from an obviously agitated Jacob Earl. And he had positively seen Mrs. Luke Hawks going past in a brand-new car, with a young man at the wheel who seemed to be teaching her to drive. Whew!

There would be a lot to tell his wife tonight.

His reflections were cut short as he strode past Henry Jones' back yard, which lay on his homeward short-cut route.

A crowd of townsfolk were gathered about the door in the fence around the yard, and Dr. Norcross could observe others in the house, peering out the windows.

Henry and Jake Harrison, mopping their faces with fatigue, stood outside peering into the yard through the cautiously opened doorway. And over the fence itself, he was able to see the tossing heads of many ponies, while their squeals cut the evening air.

"Well, Henry"—that was Martha, who came around the corner of the house and pushed through the crowd about her husband—"you've rounded up all the horses all right. But how're you going to pay for the damage they did today? Now you'll have to go to work, in spite of yourself. Even if they aren't good for anything else they've accomplished *that!*"

There was an excitement on Henry's face Dr. Norcross had never seen there before.

"Sure, Martha, sure," he agreed. "I know I'll have to pay off the damage. But Jake and me, we've got plans for these hooved jackrabbits. Know what we're going to do?"

He turned, so all of the gathered crowd could hear his announcement.

"Jake and me, we're going to use that land of Jake's south

of town to breed polo ponies!" he declared. "Yes, sir, we're going to cross these streaks of lightning with real polo ponies. We're gonna get a new breed with the speed of a whippet, the endurance of a mule, and the intelligence of a human.

"Anybody who seen these creatures skedaddle around town today knows that when we get a polo pony with their blood in it developed, it'll be something! Yes, sir, something! I wish—

"No I don't! I don't wish anything! Not a single, solitary thing! I'm not gonna wish for anything ever again, either!"

Norcross grinned. Maybe Henry had something there.

Then, noting that the sun had just vanished, he was home.

Up in his room, Danny Norcross woke groggily from a slumber that had been full of dreams. Half asleep still, he groped for and found the little piece of ivory he had kept beside him ever since he had fallen asleep the night before.

His brow wrinkled. He had been on the stair, listening to the grownups talk. They had said a lot of queer things. About horses, and money, and pictures. Then he had gotten back in bed. And played with his bit of ivory for a while. Then he had had a funny thought, and sort of a wish—

The wish that had passed through his mind, as he had been falling asleep, had been that all the things Dad and Mom and the others had said would come true, because it would be so funny if they did.

So he had wished that just for one day, maybe, all Henry Jones' wishes would be horses, and money would stick to Luke Hawks' fingers, and Jacob Earl would touch something that would coin money for somebody else for a change.

And, too, that Netty Peters' tongue really would be hinged in the middle and wag at both ends, and Mrs. Benson have two faces, and Mrs. Norton swell up and blow around like a balloon.

And that Miss Wilson would really be as pretty as a

picture, and you could truly hear silver bells when Miss Avery talked.

That had been his wish.

But now, wide-awake and staring out the window at a sky all red because the sun had set, he couldn't quite remember it, try as he would. . . .

Crouched in her darkened room, Minerva Benson felt the back of her head for the hundredth time. First with shuddering horror, then with hope, then with incredulous relief. The dreadful face was gone now.

But she would remember it, and be haunted by it forever in her dreams.

Netty Peters stared at herself in her mirror, her eyes wide and frightened. Slowly she took her hands from her throat. The queer fluttering was gone. She could talk again without that terrible voice interrupting.

But always after, when she began to speak, she would stop abruptly for fear it might sound again, in the middle of a sentence.

"I've decided, Luke," Mrs. Luke Hawks said with decision, "that we'll have the house painted and put in a new furnace. Then I'm going to take the children off on a little vacation.

"No, don't say anything! Remember, the money is in my name now, and I can spend it all, if I've a mind to. I can take it and go away to California, or any place.

"And no matter what you say or do, I'm not going to give it back!"

Jacob Earl uttered a groan. The last gold ingot had just vanished from the floor of his library.

John Wiggins turned. The tiny *chink-chink* that had sounded all afternoon had ceased. The little god still grinned, but the coins were no longer coming from his mouth.

"He's quit," the little man announced to the flushed and radiant Alice Wilson. "But we don't care. Look how much money came out of him. Why there must be fifteen thousand dollars there!

"Alice, we'll take a trip around the world. And we'll take him back to China, where he came from. He deserves a reward."

With the red afterglow tinting the little lake beside which he had parked the car, Bill Morrow turned. His arm was already about Janice Avery's shoulders.

So it really wasn't any effort for him to draw her closer and kiss her, firmly, masterfully.

The door to Danny's room opened. He heard Dad and Mom come in, and pretended for a minute that he was asleep.

"He's been napping all day," Mom was saying. "He hardly woke up enough to eat breakfast. I guess he must have lain awake late last night. But his fever was down, and he didn't seem restless, so I didn't call you."

"We'll see how he is now," Dad's voice answered; and Danny, who had closed his eyes to try to remember better, opened them again.

Dad was bending over his bed.

"How do you feel, son?" he asked.

"I feel swell," Danny told him, and struggled to a sitting position. "Look what I found yesterday in my box. What is it, Dad?"

Doctor Norcross took the piece of ivory Danny held out, and looked at it.

"I'll be darned!" he exclaimed to his wife. "Danny's found the old Chinese talisman Grandfather Jonas brought back on the last voyage of the *Yankee Star*. He gave it to me thirty years ago. Told me it had belonged to a Chinese magician.

"Its peculiar power, he said, was that if you held it tight, you could have one wish come true, providing—as the Chinese inscription on the bottom says—your mind was pure, your spirit innocent, and your motive unselfish.

"I wished on it dozens of times, but nothing ever happened. Guess it was because I was too materialistic and wished for bicycles and things.

"Here, Danny, you can keep it. But take good care of it. It's very old; even the man who gave it to Grandfather Jonas didn't know how old it was."

Danny took back the talisman.

"I made a wish, Dad," he confessed.

"So?" Dad grinned. "Did it come true?"

"I don't know," Danny admitted. "I can't remember what it was."

Dad chuckled.

"Then I guess it didn't come true," he remarked. "Never mind; you can make another. And if that one doesn't happen either, don't fret. You can keep the talisman and tell people the story. It's a good story, even if it isn't so."

Probably it wasn't so. It was certain that the next time Danny wished, nothing happened. Nor any of the times after that. So that by and by he gave up trying.

He was always a little sorry, though, that he never could remember that first wish, made when he was almost asleep.

But he never could. Not even later, when he heard people remarking how much marriage had improved Alice Wilson's appearance and how silvery Mrs. Bob Morrow's voice was.

The Truth About Pyecraft

H. G. Wells

He sits not a dozen yards away. If I glance over my shoulder I can see him. And if I catch his eye—and usually I catch his eye—it meets me with an expression——

It is mainly an imploring look—and yet with suspicion in it.

Confound his suspicion! If I wanted to tell on him I should have told long ago. I don't tell and I don't tell, and he ought to feel at his ease. As if anything so gross and fat as he could feel at ease! Who would believe me if I did tell?

Poor old Pyecraft! Great, uneasy jelly of substance! The fattest clubman in London.

He sits at one of the little club tables in the huge bay by the fire, stuffing. What is he stuffing? I glance judiciously and catch him biting at the round of hot buttered teacake, with his eyes on me. Confound him!—with his eyes on me!

That settles it, Pyecraft! Since you *will* be abject, since you *will* behave as though I was not a man of honor, here, right under your embedded eyes, I write the thing down—the plain

120

truth about Pyecraft. The man I helped, the man I shielded, and who has requited me by making my club unendurable, absolutely unendurable, with his liquid appeal, with the perpetual "don't tell" of his looks.

And, besides, why does he keep on eternally eating?

Well, here goes for the truth, the whole truth, and nothing but the truth!

Pyecraft——I made the acquaintance of Pyecraft in this very smoking-room. I was a young, nervous new member, and he saw it. I was sitting all alone, wishing I knew more of the members. Suddenly he came, a great rolling front of chins and abdomina, towards me, and grunted and sat down in a chair close by me and wheezed, scraped with a match and lit a cigar, and then addressed me. I forget what he said—something about the matches not lighting properly. Afterwards as he talked he kept stopping the waiters one by one as they went by, and telling them about the matches in that thin, fluty voice he has. But, anyhow, it was in some such way we began our talking.

He talked about various things and came round to games. And thence to my figure and complexion. "You ought to be a good cricketer," he said. I suppose I am slender, and I suppose I am rather dark, still—I am not ashamed of having a Hindu great-grandmother, but, for all that, I don't want casual strangers to see through me at a glance to *her*. So that I was set against Pyecraft from the beginning.

But he only talked about me in order to get to himself.

"I expect," he said, "you take no more exercise than I do, and probably you eat no less." (Like all excessively obese people he fancied he ate nothing.) "Yet"—and he smiled an oblique smile—"we differ."

And then he began to talk about his fatness and his fatness; all he did for his fatness and all he was going to do for his fatness; what people had advised him to do for his fatness and what he had heard of people doing for fatness similar to his. It was stifling. It was dumpling talk. It made me feel swelled to hear him.

One stands that sort of thing once in a while at a club, but a time came when I fancied I was standing too much. He took to me altogether too conspicuously. I could never go into the smoking-room but he would come wallowing towards me, and sometimes he came round while I had my lunch. He seemed at times almost to be clinging to me. He was a bore, but not so fearful a bore as to be limited to me; and from the first there was something in his manner—almost as though he knew, almost as though he penetrated to the fact that I *might*—that there was a remote, exceptional chance in me that no one else presented.

"I'd give anything to get it down," he would say—"anything," and peer at me over his vast cheeks and pant.

Poor old Pyecraft! He has just rung the bell, no doubt to order another buttered teacake!

He came to the actual thing one day. "Our Pharma-copœia," he said, "our Western Pharmacopœia, is anything but the last word of medical science. In the East, I've been told——"

He stopped and stared at me. It was like being at an aquarium.

I was quite suddenly angry with him. "Look here," I said, "who told you about my great-grandmother's recipes?"

"Well," he fenced.

"Every time we've met for a week," I said—"and we've met pretty often—you've given me a broad hint or so about that little secret of mine."

"Well," he said, "now the cat's out of the bag, I'll admit, yes, it is so. I had it——"

"From Pattison?"

"Indirectly," he said, which I believe was lying, "yes."

"Pattison," I said, "took that stuff at his own risk."

He pursed his mouth and bowed.

"My great-grandmother's recipes," I said, "are queer things to handle. My father was near making me promise——"

"He didn't?"

"No. But he warned me. He himself used one—once."

"Ah! . . . But do you think——? Suppose—suppose there did happen to be one——"

"The things are curious documents," I said. "Even the smell of 'em. . . . No!"

But after going so far Pyecraft was resolved I should go further. I was always a little afraid that if I tried his patience too much he would fall on me suddenly and smother me. I own I was weak. But I was also annoyed with Pyecraft. I had got to that state of feeling for him that disposed me to say, "Well, *take* the risk!" The little affair of Pattison to which I have alluded was a different matter altogether. What it was doesn't concern us now, but I knew, anyhow, that the particular recipe I used then was safe. The rest I didn't know so much about, and, on the whole, I was inclined to doubt their safety pretty completely.

Yet even if Pyecraft got poisoned——

I must confess the poisoning of Pyecraft struck me as an immense undertaking.

That evening I took that queer, odd-scented sandalwood box out of my safe and turned the rustling skins over. The gentleman who wrote the recipes for my great-grandmother evidently had a weakness for skins of a miscellaneous origin, and his handwriting was cramped to the last degree. Some of the things are quite unreadable to me—though my family, with its Indian Civil Service associations, has kept up a knowledge of Hindustani from generation to generation—and none are absolutely plain sailing. But I found the one that I knew was there soon enough, and sat on the floor by my safe for some time looking at it.

"Look here," said I to Pyecraft next day, and snatched the slip away from his eager grasp.

"So far as I can make it out, this is a recipe for Loss of Weight." ("Ah!" said Pyecraft.) "I'm not absolutely sure, but I think it's that. And if you take my advice you'll leave it alone. Because, you know, my ancestors on that side were, so far as I can gather, a jolly queer lot. See?"

"Let me try it," said Pyecraft.

I leaned back in my chair. My imagination made one mighty effort and fell flat within me. "What in Heaven's name, Pyecraft," I asked, "do you think you'll look like when you get thin?"

He was impervious to reason. I made him promise never to say a word to me about his disgusting fatness again whatever happened. And then I handed him that little piece of skin.

"It's nasty stuff," I said.

"No matter," he said, and took it.

He goggled at it. "But—but——" he said.

He had just discovered that it wasn't English.

"To the best of my ability," I said, "I will do you a translation."

I did my best. After that we didn't speak for a fortnight. Whenever he approached me I frowned and motioned him away, and he respected our compact. But at the end of the fortnight he was as fat as ever. And then he got a word in.

"I must speak," he said. "It isn't fair. There's something wrong. It's done me no good. You're not doing your great-grandmother justice."

"Where's the recipe?"

He produced it gingerly from his pocket-book.

I ran my eye over the items. "Was the egg addled?" I asked.

"No. Ought it to have been?"

"That," I said, "goes without saying in all my poor dear great-grandmother's recipes. When condition or quality is not specified you must get the worst. She was drastic or nothing.

. . . And there's one or two possible alternatives to some of these other things. You got *fresh* rattlesnake venom?"

"I got rattlesnake from Jamrach's. It cost—it cost——"

"That's your affair, anyhow. This last item——"

"I know a man who——"

"Yes. H'm. Well, I'll write the alternatives down. So far as I know the language, the spelling of this recipe is particularly atrocious. By-the-bye, dog here probably means pariah dog."

For a month after that I saw Pyecraft constantly at the club and as fat and anxious as ever. He kept our treaty, but at times he broke the spirit of it by shaking his head despondently. Then one day in the cloak-room he said, "Your great-grandmother——"

"Not a word against her," I said: and he held his peace.

I could have fancied he had desisted, and I saw him one day talking to three new members about his fatness as though he was in search of other recipes. And then, quite unexpectedly his telegram came.

"Mr. Formalyn!" bawled a page-boy under my nose and I took the telegram and opened it at once.

"For Heaven's sake come.—Pyecraft."

"H'm," said I, and to tell the truth I was so pleased at the rehabilitation of my great-grandmother's reputation this evidently promised that I made a most excellent lunch.

I got Pyecraft's address from the hall porter. Pyecraft inhabited the upper half of a house in Bloomsbury, and I went there as soon as I had finished my coffee. I did not wait to finish my cigar.

"Mr. Pyecraft?" said I, at the front door.

They believed he was ill; he hadn't been out for two days.

"He expects me," said I, and they sent me up.

I rang the bell at the lattice-door upon the landing.

"He shouldn't have tried it, anyhow," I said to myself. "A man who eats like a pig ought to look like a pig."

An obviously worthy woman, with an anxious face and a

carelessly placed cap, came and surveyed me through the lattice.

I gave my name and she opened his door for me in a dubious fashion.

"Well?" said I, as we stood together inside Pyecraft's piece of the landing.

"'E said you was to come in if you came," she said, and regarded me, making no motion to show me anywhere. And then, confidentially. "'E's locked in, sir."

"Locked in?"

"Locked himself in yesterday morning and 'asn't let anyone in since, sir. And ever and again *swearing*. Oh, my!"

I stared at the door she indicated by her glances. "In there?" I said.

"Yes, sir."

"What's up?"

She shook her head sadly. "'E keeps on calling for vittles, sir. '*Eavy* vittles 'e wants. I get 'im what I can. Pork 'e's 'ad, sooit puddin', sossiges, noo bread. Everythink like that. Left outside, if you please, and me go away. 'E's eatin' sir, somethink *awful*."

There came a piping bawl from inside the door: "That Formalyn?"

"'That you, Pyecraft?" I shouted, and went and banged the door.

"Tell her to go away."

I did.

Then I could hear a curious pattering upon the door, almost like someone feeling for the handle in the dark, and Pyecraft's familiar grunts.

"It's all right," I said, "she's gone."

But for a long time the door didn't open.

I heard the key turn. Then Pyecraft's voice said, "Come in."

I turned the handle and opened the door. Naturally I expected to see Pyecraft.

Well, you know, he wasn't there!

I never had such a shock in my life. There was his sitting room in a state of untidy disorder, plates and dishes among the books and writing things, and several chairs overturned, but Pyecraft——

"It's all right, old man; shut the door," he said, and then I discovered him.

There he was right up close to the cornice in the corner by the door, as though someone had glued him to the ceiling. His face was anxious and angry. He panted and gesticulated. "Shut the door," he said. "If that woman gets hold of it——"

I shut the door, and went and stood away from him and stared.

"If anything gives way and you tumble down," I said, "you'll break your neck, Pyecraft."

"I wish I could," he wheezed.

"A man of your age and weight getting up there to do kiddish gymnastics——"

"Don't," he said, and looked agonized. "Your great-grand-mother——"

"Be careful," I warned him.

"I'll tell you," he said, and gesticulated.

"How the deuce," said I, "are you holding on up there?"

And then abruptly I realized that he was not holding on at all, that he was floating up there—just as a gas-filled bladder might have floated in the same position. He began a struggle to thrust himself away from the ceiling and to clamber down the wall to me. "It's that prescription," he panted, as he did so. "Your great-gran——"

"*No!*" I cried.

He took hold of a framed engraving rather carelessly as he spoke and it gave way, and he flew back to the ceiling again, while the picture smashed on to the sofa. He tried again more carefully, coming down by way of the mantel.

It was really a most extraordinary spectacle, that great, fat,

apoplectic-looking man upside down and trying to get from the ceiling to the floor. "That prescription," he said. "Too successful."

"How?"

"Loss of weight—almost complete."

And then, of course, I understood.

"By Jove, Pyecraft," said I, "what you wanted was a cure for fatness! But you always called it weight. You would call it weight."

Somehow I was extremely delighted. I quite liked Pyecraft just then. "Let me help you!" I said, and took his hand and pulled him down. He kicked about, trying to get a foothold somewhere. It was very like holding a flag on a windy day.

"That table," he said, pointing, "is solid mahogany and very heavy. If you can put me under that——"

I did, and there he wallowed about like a captive balloon, while I stood on his hearthrug and talked to him.

I lit a cigar. "Tell me," I said, "what happened?"

"I took it," he said.

"How did it taste?"

"Oh, *beastly!*"

I should fancy they all did. Whether one regards the ingredients or the probable compound or the possible results, almost all my great-grandmother's remedies appear to me at least to be extraordinarily uninviting. For my own part——

"I took a little sip first."

"Yes?"

"And as I felt lighter and better after an hour, I decided to take the draught."

"My dear Pyecraft!"

"I held my nose," he explained. "And then I kept on getting lighter and lighter—and helpless, you know."

He gave way suddenly to a burst of passion. "What am I to *do?*" he said.

"There's one thing pretty evident," I said, "that you musn't do. If you go out of doors you'll go up and up." I waved an arm upward. "They'd have to send Santos-Dumont after you to bring you down again."

"I suppose it will wear off?"

I shook my head. "I don't think you can count on that," I said.

And then there was another burst of passion, and he kicked out at adjacent chairs and banged the floor. He behaved just as I should have expected a great, fat, self-indulgent man to behave under trying circumstances—that is to say, very badly. He spoke of me and of my great-grandmother with an utter want of discretion.

"I never asked you to take the stuff," I said.

And generously disregarding the insults he was putting upon me, I sat down in his armchair and began to talk to him in a sober, friendly fashion.

I pointed out to him that this was a trouble he had brought upon himself, and that it had almost an air of poetical justice. He had eaten too much. This he disputed, and for a time we argued the point.

He became noisy and violent, so I desisted from this aspect of his lesson. "And then," said I, "you committed the sin of euphemism. You called it, not Fat, which is just and inglorious, but Weight. You——"

He interrupted to say that he recognized all that. What was he to *do?*

I suggested he should adapt himself to his new conditions. So we came to the really sensible part of the business. I suggested that it would not be difficult for him to learn to walk about on the ceiling with his hands——

"I can't sleep," he said.

But that was no great difficulty. It was quite possible, I pointed out, to make a shake-up under a wire mattress, fasten the under things on with tapes, and have a blanket, sheet, and coverlid to button at the side. He would have to confide in his housekeeper, I said; and after some squabbling he agreed to that. (Afterwards it was quite delightful to see the beautifully matter-of-fact way with which the good lady took all these amazing inversions.) He could have a library ladder in his room, and all his meals could be laid on the top of his bookcase. We also hit on an ingenious device by which he could get to the floor whenever he wanted, which was simply to put the *British Encyclopædia* on the top of his open shelves. He just pulled out a couple of volumes and held on, and down he came. And we agreed there must be iron staples along the skirting, so that he could cling to those whenever he wanted to get about the room on the lower level.

As we got on with the thing I found myself almost keenly interested. It was I who called in the housekeeper and broke matters to her, and it was I chiefly who fixed up the inverted bed. In fact, I spent two whole days at his flat. I am a handy, interfering sort of man with a screwdriver, and I made all sorts of ingenious adaptations for him—ran a wire to bring his bells within reach, turned all his electric lights up instead of down, and so on. The whole affair was extremely curious and interesting to me, and it was delightful to think of Pyecraft like some great, fat blow-fly, crawling about on his ceiling and clambering round the lintel of his doors from one room to another, and never, never, never coming to the club any more. . . .

Then, you know, my fatal ingenuity got the better of me. I was sitting by his fire, and he was up in his favorite corner by the cornice, tacking a Turkey carpet to the ceiling, when the idea struck me. "By Jove, Pyecraft!" I said. "All this is totally unnecessary."

And before I could calculate the complete consequences of my notion I blurted it out. "Lead underclothing," said I, and the mischief was done.

Pyecraft received the thing almost in tears. "To be right ways up again——" he said.

I gave him the whole secret before I saw where it would take me. "Buy sheet lead," I said, "stamp it into discs. Sew 'em all over your underclothes until you have enough. Have lead-soled boots, carry a bag of solid lead, and the thing is done! Instead of being a prisoner here you may go abroad again, Pycraft! you may travel——"

A still happier idea came to me. "You need never fear a shipwreck. All you need do is just slip off some or all of your clothes, take the necessary amount of luggage in your hand, and float up in the air——"

In his emotion he dropped the tack-hammer within an inch of my head. "By Jove!" he said. "I shall be able to come back to the club again."

The thing pulled me up short. "By Jove!" I said, faintly. "Yes. Of course—you will."

He did. He does. There he sits behind me now stuffing—as I live!—a third go of buttered teacake. And no one in the whole world knows—except his housekeeper and me—that he weighs practically nothing. There he sits watching until I have done this writing. Then, if he can, he will waylay me. He will come billowing up to me. . . .

He will tell me over again all about it, how it feels, how it doesn't feel, how he sometimes hopes it is passing off a little. And always somewhere in that fat, abundant discourse he will say, "The secret's keeping, eh? If anyone knew of it—I should be so ashamed. . . . Makes a fellow look such a fool, you know. Crawling about on a ceiling and all that. . . ."

And now to elude Pyecraft, occupying, as he does, an admirable strategic position between me and the door.

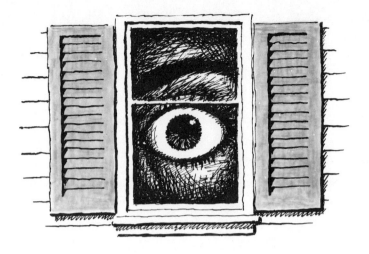

Housing Problem

Henry Kuttner

Jacqueline said it was a canary, but I contended that there were a couple of lovebirds in the covered cage. One canary could never make that much fuss. Besides, I liked to think of crusty old Mr. Henchard keeping lovebirds; it was so completely inappropriate. But whatever our roomer kept in that cage by his window, he shielded it—or them—jealously from prying eyes. All we had to go by were the noises.

And they weren't too simple to figure out. From under the cretonne cloth came shufflings, rustlings, occasional faint and inexplicable pops, and once or twice a tiny thump that made the whole hidden cage shake on its redwood pedestal-stand. Mr. Henchard must have known that we were curious. But all he said, when Jackie remarked that birds were nice to have around, was "Claptrap! Leave that cage alone, d'ya hear?"

That made us a little mad. We're not snoopers, and after that brushoff, we coldly refused even to look at the shrouded cretonne shape. We didn't want to lose Mr. Henchard, either. Roomers were surprisingly hard to get. Our little house was

133

on the coast highway. The town was a couple of dozen homes, a grocery, a liquor store, the post office, and Terry's restaurant. That was about all. Every morning Jackie and I hopped the bus and rode in to the factory, an hour away. By the time we got home we were pretty tired. We couldn't get any household help—war jobs paid a lot better—so we both pitched in and cleaned. As for cooking, we were Terry's best customers.

The wages were good, but before the war we'd run up too many debts, so we needed extra money. And that's why we rented a room to Mr. Henchard. Off the beaten track with transportation difficult, and with the coast dimout every night, it wasn't too easy to get a roomer. Mr. Henchard looked like a natural. He was, we figured, too old to get into mischief.

One day he wandered in, paid a deposit; presently he showed up with a huge Gladstone and a square canvas grip with leather handles. He was a creaking little old man with a bristling tonsure of stiff white hair and a face like Popeye's father, only more human. He wasn't sour; he was just crusty. I had a feeling he'd spent most of his life in furnished rooms, minding his own business and puffing innumerable cigarettes through a long black holder. But he wasn't one of those lonely old men you could safely feel sorry for—far from it! He wasn't poor and he was completely self-sufficient. We loved him. I called him grandpa once, in an outburst of affection, and my skin blistered at the resultant remarks.

Some people are born under lucky stars. Mr. Henchard was like that. He was always finding money in the street. The few times we played poker, he held straights without even trying. No question of sharp dealing—he was just lucky.

I remember the time we were all going down the long wooden stairway that leads from the cliff-top to the beach. Mr. Henchard kicked at a pretty big rock that was on one of the steps. The stone bounced down a little way, and then went right through one of the treads. The wood was completely rotten. We felt fairly certain that if Mr. Henchard, who was leading, had stepped on that rotten section, the whole thing would have collapsed.

And then there was the time I was riding up with him in the bus. The motor stopped a few minutes after we'd boarded the bus; the driver pulled over. A car was coming toward us along the highway and, as we stopped, one of its front tires blew out. It skidded into the ditch. If we hadn't stopped when we did, there would have been a head-on collision. Not a soul was hurt.

Mr. Henchard wasn't lonely; he went out by day, I think, and at night he sat in his room near the window most of the time. We knocked, of course, before coming in to clean, and sometimes he'd say, "Wait a minute." There'd be a hasty rustling and the sound of that cretonne cover going on his bird cage. We wondered what sort of bird he had, and theorized on the possibility of a phoenix. The creature never sang. It made noises. Soft, odd, not-always-birdlike noises. By the time we got home from work, Mr. Henchard was always in his room. He stayed there while we cleaned. On weekends, he never went out.

As for the cage . . .

One night Mr. Henchard came out, stuffing a cigarette into his holder, and looked us over.

"Mph," said Mr. Henchard. "Listen, I've got some property to 'tend to up north, and I'll be away for a week or so. I'll still pay the rent."

"Oh, well," Jackie said. "We can—"

"Claptrap," he growled. "It's my room. I'll keep it if I like. How about that, hey?"

We agreed, and he smoked half his cigarette in one gasp. "Mm-m. Well, look here, now. Always before I've had my own car. So I've taken my bird cage with me. This time I've got to travel on the bus, so I can't take it. You've been pretty nice—not peepers or pryers. You got sense. I'm going to leave my bird cage here, but *don't you touch that cover!*"

"The canary—" Jackie gulped. "It'll starve."

"Canary, hmm?" Mr. Henchard said, fixing her with a beady, wicked eye. "Never you mind. I left plenty o' food *and* water. You just keep your hands off. Clean my room when it needs it, if you want, but don't you dare touch the bird cage. What do you say?"

"Okay with us," I said.

"Well, you mind what I say," he snapped.

That next night, when we got home, Mr. Henchard was gone. We went into his room and there was a note pinned to the cretonne cover. It said, "Mind, now!" Inside the cage something went *rustle-whirr*. And then there was a faint pop.

"Let's forget it," I said. "Want the shower first?"

"Yes," Jackie said.

Whirr-r went the cage. But it wasn't wings. *Thump!*

The next night I said, "Maybe he left enough food, but I bet the water's getting low."

"Eddie!" Jackie remarked.

"All right, I'm curious. But I don't like the idea of birds dying of thirst, either."

"Mr. Henchard said—"

"All right, again. Let's go down to Terry's and see what the lamb chop situation is."

The next night—Oh, well. We lifted the cretonne. I still think we were less curious than worried. Jackie said she once knew somebody who used to beat his canary.

"We'll find the poor beast cowering in chains," she remarked, flicking her dust-cloth at the windowsill, behind the cage. I turned off the vacuum. *Whish—trot-trot-trot* went something under the cretonne.

"Yeah—" I said. "Listen, Jackie. Mr. Henchard's all right, but he's a crackpot. That bird or birds may be thirsty now. I'm going to take a look."

"No. Uh—yes. We both will, Eddie. We'll split the responsibility."

I reached for the cover, and Jackie ducked under my arm and put her hand over mine.

Then we lifted a corner of the cloth. Something had been rustling around inside, but the instant we touched the cretonne, the sound stopped. I meant to take only one swift glance. My hand continued to lift the cover, though. I could see my arm moving and I couldn't stop it. I was too busy looking.

Inside the cage was a—well, a little house. It seemed complete in every detail. A tiny house painted white, with green shutters—ornamental, not meant to close—for the cottage was strictly modern. It was the sort of comfortable, well-built house you see all the time in the suburbs. The tiny windows had chintz curtains; they were lighted up, on the ground floor. The moment we lifted the cloth, each window suddenly blacked out. The lights didn't go off, but shades snapped down with an irritated jerk. It happened fast. Neither of us saw who or what pulled down those shades.

I let go of the cover and stepped back, pulling Jackie with me.

"A d-doll house, Eddie!"

"With dolls in it?"

I stared past her at the hooded cage. "Could you, maybe, do you think, perhaps, train a canary to pull down shades?"

"Oh, my! Eddie, listen."

Faint sounds were coming from the cage. Rustles, and an almost inaudible pop. Then a scraping.

I went over and took the cretonne cloth clear off. This time I was ready; I watched the windows. But the shades flicked down as I blinked.

Jackie touched my arm and pointed. On the sloping roof was a miniature brick chimney; a wisp of pale smoke was rising from it. The smoke kept coming up, but it was so thin I couldn't even smell it.

"The c-canaries are c-cooking," Jackie gurgled.

We stood there for a while, expecting almost anything. If a

little green man had popped out of the front door and offered us three wishes, we shouldn't have been much surprised. Only nothing happened.

There wasn't a sound, now, from the wee house in the bird cage.

And the blinds were down. I could see that the whole affair was a masterpiece of detail. The little front porch had a tiny mat on it. There was a doorbell, too.

Most cages have removable bottoms. This one didn't. Resin-stains and dull gray metal showed where soldering had been done. The door was soldered shut, too. I could put my forefinger between the bars, but my thumb was too thick.

"It's a nice little cottage, isn't it?" Jackie said, her voice quavering. "They must be such *little* guys—"

"Guys?"

"Birds. Eddie, who lives in that house?"

"Well," I said. I took out my automatic pencil, gently inserted it between the bars of the cage, and poked at an open window, where the shade snapped up. From within the house something like the needlebeam of a miniature flashlight shot into my eye, blinding me with its brilliance. As I grunted and jerked back, I heard a window slam and the shade come down again.

"Did you see what happened?"

"No, your head was in the way. But—"

As we looked, the lights went out. Only the thin smoke curling from the chimney indicated that anything was going on.

"Mr. Henchard's a mad scientist," Jackie muttered. "He shrinks people."

"Not without an atom-smasher," I said. "Every mad scientist's got to have an atom-smasher to make artificial lightning."

I put my pencil between the bars again. I aimed carefully, pressed the point against the doorbell, and rang. A thin shrilling was heard.

The shade at one of the windows by the door was twitched aside hastily, and something probably looked at me. I don't know. I wasn't quick enough to see it. The shade fell back in place, and there was no more movement. I rang the bell till I got tired of it. Then I stopped.

"I could take the cage apart," I said.

"Oh, *no!* Mr. Henchard—"

"Well," I said, "when he comes back, I'm going to ask him what this is all about. He can't keep pixies. It isn't in the lease."

"He doesn't have a lease," Jackie countered.

I examined the little house in the bird cage. No sound, no movement. Smoke coming from the chimney.

After all, we had no right to break into the cage. House-breaking? I had visions of a little green man with wings flourishing a night-stick, arresting me for burglary. Did pixies have cops? What sort of crimes . . .

I put the cover back on the cage. After a while, vague noises emerged. *Scrape. Thump. Rustle, rustle, rustle. Pop.* And an unbirdlike trilling that broke off short.

"Oh, my," Jackie said. "Let's go away quick."

We went right to bed. I dreamed of a horde of little green guys in cop uniforms, dancing on a bilious rainbow and singing gaily.

The alarm clock woke me. I showered, shaved and dressed, thinking of the same thing Jackie was thinking of. As we put on our coats, I met her eyes and said, "Shall we?"

"Yes. Oh, golly, Eddie! D-do you suppose they'll be leaving for work, too?"

"What sort of work?" I inquired angrily. "Painting buttercups?"

There wasn't a sound from beneath the cretonne when we tiptoed into Mr. Henchard's room. Morning sunlight blazed through the window. I jerked the cover off. There was the house. One of the blinds was up; all the rest were tightly firm. I put my head close to the cage and stared through the bars into the open window, where scraps of chintz curtains were blowing in the breeze.

I saw a great big eye looking back at me.

This time Jackie was certain I'd got my mortal wound. The breath went out of her with a whoosh as I caromed back, yelling about a horrible blood-shot eye that wasn't human. We clutched each other for a while and then I looked again.

"Oh," I said, rather faintly. "It's a mirror."

"A *mirror?*" she gasped.

"Yeah, a big one, on the opposite wall. That's all I can see. I can't get close enough to the window."

"Look on the porch," Jackie said.

I looked. There was a milk bottle standing by the door— you can guess the size of it. It was purple. Beside it was a folded postage stamp.

"Purple milk?" I said.

"From a purple cow. Or else the bottle's colored. Eddie, is that a newspaper?"

It was. I strained my eyes to read the headlines. EXTRA was splashed redly across the sheet, in huge letters nearly a sixteenth of an inch high. EXTRA—FOTZPA MOVES ON TUR! That was all we could make out.

I put the cretonne gently back over the cage. We went down to Terry's for breakfast while we waited for the bus.

When we rode home that night, we knew what our first job would be. We let ourselves into the house, discovered that Mr. Henchard hadn't come back yet, switched on the light in his room, and listened to the noises from the bird cage.

"Music," Jackie said.

It was so faint I scarcely heard it, and, in any case, it wasn't real music. I can't begin to describe it. And it died away immediately. *Thump, scrape, pop, buzz.* Then silence, and I pulled off the cover.

The house was dark, the windows were shut, the blinds

were down. Paper and milk bottle were gone from the porch. On the front door was a sign that said—after I used a magnifying glass: QUARANTINE! SCOPPY FEVER!

"Why, the little liars," I said. "I bet they haven't got scoppy fever at all."

Jackie giggled wildly. "You only get scoppy fever in April, don't you?"

"April and Christmas. That's when the bread-and-butter flies carry it. Where's my pencil?"

I rang the bell. A shade twitched aside, flipped back; neither of us had seen the—hand?—that moved it. Silence; no smoke coming out of the chimney.

"Scared?" I asked.

"No. It's funny, but I'm not. They're such standoffish little guys."

"They can't snoot us this way," I said. "It's our house their house is in, if you follow me."

"What can we do?"

I manipulated the pencil, and, with considerable difficulty, wrote LET US IN on the white panel of the door. There wasn't room for more than that. Jackie tsked.

"Maybe you shouldn't have written that. We don't want to get *in*. We just want to see them."

"Too late now. Besides, they'll know what we mean."

We stood watching the house in the bird cage, and it watched us, in a sullen and faintly annoyed fashion. SCOPPY FEVER, indeed!

That was all that happened that night.

The next morning we found that the tiny front door had been scrubbed clean of my pencil marks, that the quarantine sign was still there, and that there was a bottle of green milk and another paper on the porch. This time the headline said: EXTRA—FOTZPA OVERSHOOTS TUR!

Smoke was idling from the chimney. I rang the bell again. No answer. I noticed a domino of a mailbox by the door, chiefly because I could see through the slot that there were letters inside. But the thing was locked.

"If we could see whom they were addressed to—" Jackie suggested.

"Or whom they're from. That's what interests me."

Finally, we went to work. I was preoccupied all day, and nearly welded my thumb onto a boggie-arm. When I met Jackie that night, I could see that she'd been bothered, too.

"Let's ignore them," she said as we bounced home on the bus. "We know when we're not wanted, don't we?"

"I'm not going to be high-hatted by a—by a critter. Besides, we'll both go quietly nuts if we don't find out what's inside that house. Do you suppose Mr. Henchard's a wizard?"

"He's a devil," Jackie said bitterly. "Going off and leaving pixies on our hands!"

When we got home, the little house in the bird cage took alarm, as usual, and by the time we'd yanked off the cover, the distant, soft noises had faded into silence. Lights shone through the drawn blinds. The porch had only the mat on it. In the mailbox we could see the yellow envelope of a telegram.

Jackie turned pale. "It's the last straw," she insisted. "A telegram!"

"It may not be."

"It is, it is, I know it is. Aunt Tinker Bell's dead. Or Iolanthe's coming for a visit."

"The quarantine sign's off the door," I said. "There's a new one. It says 'wet paint.'"

"Well, you will scribble all over their nice clean door."

I put the cretonne back, turned off the light-switch, and took Jackie's hand. We stood waiting. After a time something went *bump-bump-bump,* and then there was a singing, like a tea-kettle. I heard a tiny clatter.

Next morning there were twenty-six bottles of yellow milk

—bright yellow—on the tiny porch, and the Lilliputian head-line announced: EXTRA—TUR SLIDES TOWARD FOTZPA! There was mail in the box, too, but the telegram was gone.

That night things continued much as before. When I pulled the cloth off there was a sudden, furious silence. We felt that we were being watched around the corners of the miniature shades. We finally went to bed, but in the middle of the night I got up and took another look at our mysterious tenants. Not that I saw *them*, of course. But they must have been throwing a party, for bizarre, small music and wild thumps and pops died into silence as I peeked.

In the morning there was a red bottle and a newspaper on the little porch. The headline said: EXTRA—FOTZPA GOES UP!

"My work's going to the dogs," I said. "I can't concentrate for thinking about this business—and wondering. . . ."

"Me, too. We've *got* to find out somehow."

I peeked. A shade came down so sharply that it almost tore free from its roller.

"Do you think they're mad?" I asked.

"Yes," Jackie said, "I do. We must be bothering the very devil out of 'em. Look—I'll bet they're sitting inside by the windows, boiling mad, waiting for us to go away. Maybe we'd better go. It's time for the bus anyway."

I looked at the house, and the house, I felt, looked at me with an air of irritated and resentful fury. Oh, well. We went to work.

We were tired and hungry when we got back that night, but even before removing our coats we went into Mr. Henchard's room. Silence. I switched on the light while Jackie pulled off the cretonne cover from the cage.

I heard her gasp. Instantly I jumped forward, expecting to see a little green guy on that absurd porch—or anything, for that matter. I saw nothing unusual. There was no smoke coming from the chimney.

But Jackie was pointing to the front door. There was a neat, painted sign tacked to the panel. It said, very sedately, simply, and finally: TO LET.

"Oh, oh, oh!" Jackie said.

I gulped. All the shades were up in the tiny windows and the chintz curtains were gone. We could see into the house for the first time. It was completely and awfully empty.

No furniture, anywhere. Nothing at all but a few scrapes and scratches on the polished hardwood floor. The wallpaper was scrupulously clean; the patterns, in the various rooms, were subdued and in good taste. The tenants had left their house in order.

"They moved," I said.

"Yes," Jackie murmured. "They moved out."

All of a sudden I felt terrible. The house—not the tiny one in the cage, but our own—was awfully empty. You know how it is when you've been on a visit, and come home into a place that's full of nothing and nobody?

I grabbed Jackie and held her tight. She felt pretty bad, too. You wouldn't think that a tiny TO LET sign could make so much difference.

"What'll Mr. Henchard say?" Jackie asked, watching me with big eyes.

Mr. Henchard came home two nights later. We were sitting by the fire when he walked in, his Gladstone swinging, the black cigarette holder jutting from below his beak. "Mph," he greeted us.

"Hello," I said weakly. "Glad you're back."

"Claptrap!" said Mr. Henchard firmly as he headed for his room. Jackie and I looked at one another.

Mr. Henchard squalled in sheer fury. His twisted face appeared around the door.

"Busybodies!" he snarled. "I *told* you—"

"Wait a minute," I said.

"I'm moving out!" Mr. Henchard barked. "Now!" His head popped back out of sight; the door slammed and locked. Jackie and I waited, half expecting to be spanked.

Mr. Henchard bounced out of his room. Gladstone suspended from one hand. He whirled past us toward the door. I tried to stop him. "Mr. Henchard—"

"Claptrap!"

Jackie pulled one arm, I got a grip on the other. Between us, we managed to bring him to a stop.

"Wait," I said. "You've forgotten your—uh—bird cage."

"That's what you think," he snarled at me. "You can have it. Meddlers! It took me months to build that little house just right, and months more to coax 'em to live in it. Now you've spoiled it. They won't be back."

"Who?" Jackie gulped.

His eyes were fixed malignantly on us. "My tenants. I'll have to build a new house now—ha! But this time I won't leave it within reach of meddlers."

"Wait," I said. "Are—are you a m-magician?"

Mr. Henchard snorted. "I'm a good craftsman. That's all it takes. You treat them right, and they'll treat you right. Still—" And he gleamed a bit with pride. "—it isn't everybody who knows how to build the right sort of house for *them!*"

He seemed to be softening, but my next question aroused him again.

"What were they?" he snapped. "The Little Folk, of course. Call 'em what you like. Nixie, pixie, leprechaun, brownie—they've had lots of names. But they want a quiet, respectable neighborhood to live in, not a lot of peeping and prying. Gives the property a bad name. No wonder they moved out! And—mph!—they paid their rent on time, too. Still, the Little Folk always do," he added.

"Rent?" Jackie said faintly.

"Luck," Mr. Henchard said. "Good luck. What did you expect they'd pay in—money? Now I'll have to build another house to get my special luck back."

He gave us one parting glare, jerked open the door, and stamped out. We stood looking after him. The bus was pulling into the gas station down the slope, and Mr. Henchard broke into a run.

He caught the bus, all right, but only after he'd fallen flat on his face.

I put my arm around Jackie.

"Oh, gosh," she said. "His bad luck's working already."

"Not *bad*," I pointed out. "Just normal. When you rent a little house to pixies, you get a lot of extra good luck."

We sat in silence, watching each other. Finally without saying a word, we went into Mr. Henchard's vacated room. The bird cage was still there. So was the house. So was the TO LET sign.

"Let's go to Terry's," I said.

We stayed later than usual. Anybody would have thought we didn't want to go home because we lived in a haunted house. Except that in our case the exact opposite was true. Our house wasn't haunted any more. It was horribly, desolately, coldly vacant.

I didn't say anything till we'd crossed the highway, climbed the slope, and unlocked our front door. We went, I don't know why, for a final look at the empty house. The cover was back on the cage, where I'd replaced it, but *thump, rustle, pop!* The house was tenanted again!

We backed out and closed the door before we breathed.

"No," Jackie said. "We mustn't look. We mustn't ever, *ever*, look under that cover."

"Never," I said. "Who do you suppose. . ."

We caught a very faint murmur of what seemed to be boisterous singing. That was fine. The happier they were, the longer they'd stay. We went to bed.

It was unimportant that the next morning was rainy. We

were convinced that bright yellow sunlight was blazing in through the windows. I sang under the shower. Jackie burbled inarticulately and joyously. We didn't open Mr. Henchard's door.

"Maybe they want to sleep late," I said.

It's always noisy in the machine-shop, and a hand-truck load of rough cylinder casings going past doesn't increase the din noticeably. At three o'clock that afternoon, one of the boys was rolling the stuff along toward the storeroom, and I didn't hear it or see it until I'd stepped back from my planer, cocking my eye at its adjustment.

Those big planers are minor juggernauts. They have to be bedded in concrete, in heavy thigh-high cradles on which a heavily weighted metal monster—the planer itself—slides back and forth.

I stepped back, saw the hand-truck coming, and made a neat waltz turn to get out of its way. The boy with the hand-truck swerved, the cylinders began to fall out, and I took an unbalanced waltz step that ended with my smacking my thighs against the edge of the cradle and doing a neat, suicidal half-somersault. When I landed, I was jammed into the metal cradle, looking at the planer as it zoomed down on me. I've never in my life seen anything move so fast.

It was all over before I knew it. I was struggling to bounce myself out, men were yelling, the planer was bellowing with blood-thirsty triumph, and the cylinder heads were rolling around underfoot all over the place. Then there was the crackling, tortured crash of gears and cams going to pieces. The planer stopped. My heart started.

After I'd changed my clothes, I waited for Jackie to quit work. Rolling home on the bus, I told her about it. "Pure dumb luck. Or else a miracle. One of those cylinders bounced into the planer in just the right place. The planer's a mess, but I'm not. I think we ought to write a note of thanks to our—uh—tenants."

Jackie nodded with profound conviction. "It's the luck they

pay their rent in, Eddie. I'm glad they paid in advance, too!"

"Except that I'm off the payroll till the planer's fixed," I said.

We went home through a storm. We could hear a banging in Mr. Henchard's room, louder than any noise that had ever come from the bird cage. We rushed upstairs and found the casement window had come open. I closed it. The cretonne cover had been half blown off the cage, and I started to pull it back in place. Jackie was beside me. We looked at the tiny house; my hand didn't complete its gesture. The TO LET sign had been removed from the door. The chimney was smoking greasily. The blinds were tightly down, as usual, but there were other changes.

There was a small smell of cooking—scorned beef and skunk cabbage, I thought wildly. Unmistakably it came from the pixie house. On the formerly immaculate porch was a slopping-over garbage can, and a minuscule orange crate with unwashed, atom-sized tin cans and empty bottles. There was a milk bottle by the door, too, filled with biliously lavender liquid. It hadn't been taken in yet, nor had the morning paper. It was certainly a different paper. The lurid size of the headlines indicated that it was a yellow tabloid.

A clothesline, without any clothes hanging on it at the moment, had been tacked up from one pillar of the porch to a corner of the house.

I jerked down the cover, and fled after Jackie into the kitchen. "My God!" I said.

"We should have asked for references," she gasped. "Those aren't *our* tenants!"

"Not the tenants we used to have," I agreed. "I mean the ones Mr. Henchard used to have. Did you see that garbage-pail on the porch!"

"And the clothesline," Jackie added. "How—how sloppy." She gulped. "Mr. Henchard said they wouldn't be back, you know."

"Yeah, but, well—"

She nodded slowly, as though beginning to understand. I said, "Give."

"I don't know. Only Mr. Henchard said the Little Folk wanted a quiet, respectable neighborhood. And we drove them out. I'll bet we gave the bird cage—the location—a bad reputation. The better-class pixies won't live there. It's—oh, dear—maybe it's a slum."

"You're very nuts," I said.

"I'm not. It must be that. Mr. Henchard said as much. He told us he'd have to build a new house. Desirable tenants won't move into a bad neighborhood. We've got sloppy pixies, that's all."

My mouth opened. I stared at her.

"Uh-huh. I'll bet they keep a pixilated goat in the kitchen," Jackie babbled.

"Well," I said, "we're not going to stand for it. I'll evict 'em. I—I'll pour water down their chimney. Where's the tea-kettle?"

Jackie grabbed me. "No, you don't! We can't evict them, Eddie. We mustn't. They pay their rent," she said.

And then I remembered. "The planer—"

"Just that," Jackie emphasized, digging her fingers into my biceps. "You'd have been killed today if you hadn't had some extra good luck. Those pixies may be sloppy, but they pay their rent."

I got the angle. "Mr. Henchard's luck worked differently, though. Remember when he kicked that rock down the beach steps, and they started to cave in? Me, I do it the hard way. I fall in the planer, sure, and a cylinder bounces after me and stops the machine, but I'll be out of a job till the planer's fixed. Nothing like that ever happened to Mr. Henchard."

"He had a better class of tenant," Jackie explained, with a wild gleam in her eye. "If Mr. Henchard had fallen in the planer, a fuse would have blown. I'll bet. Our tenants are sloppy pixies, so we get sloppy luck."

"They stay," I said. "We own a slum. Let's get out of here and go down to Terry's."

We buttoned our raincoats and departed, breathing the fresh, wet air. The storm was slashing down as furiously as ever. I'd forgotten my flashlight, but I didn't want to go back for it. We headed down the slope, toward Terry's faintly visible lights.

It was dark. We couldn't see much through the storm. Probably that was why we didn't notice the bus until it was bearing down on us, headlights almost invisible in the dimout.

I started to pull Jackie aside, out of the way, but my foot slipped on the wet concrete, and we took a nosedive. I felt Jackie's body hurtle against me, and the next moment we were floundering in the muddy ditch beside the highway while the bus roared past us and was gone.

We crawled out and made for Terry's. She stared at us, and said, "Whew!"

"Unquestionably," I said, "our lives have just been saved."

"Yes," Jackie agreed, scraping mud from her ears. "But it wouldn't have happened this way to Mr. Henchard."

Terry shook her head. "Fall in the ditch, Eddie? And you too? Bad luck!"

"Not bad," Jackie told her feebly. "Good. But sloppy." She lifted her glass of water and eyed me with muddy misery. I clinked my glass against hers.

"Well," I said. "Here's luck."

In A Dim Room

Lord Dunsany

It is some while now since I have recorded any unusual experience that has come the way of my friend Jorkens. The fact is that I incurred a certain amount of odium in one house by bringing him into it. It was not my fault, nor do I think it was his. What happened was that a certain friend of mine said that his children liked thrilling tales, and I told them a few tales of lions and tigers, which had quite failed to thrill them. It suddenly occurred to me that there is something a little unusual in some of Jorkens' experiences amongst Asian or African carnivora, so that any tale of his might be likely to succeed where those that I told had failed. So I said to my friend's three children that I knew an old hunter of big game whose experiences were more out-of-the-way than mine, and asked my friend if I might one day bring him to tea.

I had no idea that there would be anything frightening about one of Jorkens' tales; nor did I think that the three children, ranging between ten and twelve years old, would be

151

easily frightened. The permission to bring Jorkens was readily given, and the children unfortunately asked him for a thrilling tale, in those actual words, and Jorkens began at once as soon as they asked him. Now it is all blamed on me. I can only say that they asked for it, and they got it.

It should be borne in mind that they had never seen Jorkens before, and had only his own word for what kind of man he was; and then children can be very credulous. Well, here is the story, which he told almost as soon as he was seated in a comfortable chair, with the children standing before him, two boys of ten and eleven and a girl of twelve.

It was all about a tiger. But I was counting on his telling a straight story, such as I have so often heard him tell to grownups, and did not expect him to vary his style to suit his audience, if "suit" can be the proper word for the alarming effect he created.

"The tiger," said Jorkens, "had spotted me and was following me quite leisurely, as though it did not want to run in the hot weather, and knew perfectly well that I couldn't. My story may serve as a convenient warning to you, when you grow up, never to go near an Indian jungle unarmed, and never to think as I did that just for once, on that particular morning, and for only a short walk, it wouldn't matter. It mattered more than I think you can possibly guess. The tiger was there, and he was coming slowly after me, and I was walking away, and the tiger was walking a little faster than I was. Well, of course I realized that, if he was only doing five yards in a hundred faster, I had no chance of escaping by walking. And I knew that running would only make it worse."

"Why?" asked the children.

"Why," said Jorkens, "because if I started a new game the tiger would play it too. At walking he was only gaining five yards in a hundred, but at running he would have gained fifty. That's why I preferred walking, but it wasn't any better really, because it would end the same way. Unfortunately it wasn't actually in the jungle, but on some rocky land outside it; and there was no chance of a tree, because I was walking away from the jungle."

"Why?" asked another child.

"Because the tiger was between me and it," said Jorkens. "The tigers go outside the jungle at night and go back in the very early morning, when the peacocks are waking and screaming. All this was in the early morning, but the sun was well up and I thought that the tigers would all have been back long ago. So I went for that walk unarmed, and of course I was quite mistaken."

"Why were you taking the walk?" asked the girl.

"You should never ask anyone," said Jorkens, "why he did anything that leads to disaster; because all such things are done for the same reason, which one does not like to admit. But there it is, they are all for the same reason, pure foolishness."

"Did it lead to disaster?" asked she.

"You shall hear," said Jorkens. "Well, I think I told you I was on rocky land; it was hilly too; and the tiger was getting nearer. And then I saw a cave in the rocks, near the top of a little hill. Of course to go in there would cut off my retreat; but my retreat was doing me no good, and there was nowhere better to go. It seemed to me that the small cave might get smaller, till there was no room for the tiger, or it might get larger and have ramifications amongst which I might dodge him. There were just two small hopes and nowhere else to go. So I stooped and went into the cave, and the tiger came in too.

"He was still some way behind me, and I saw the light go out as he entered, for he just about filled the entrance. The cave did get smaller, and soon I was on all fours. Still the tiger did not hurry. If it got smaller still, I might still conceivably squeeze on where the tiger could not. And it did get a little smaller, but not small enough. We went on over the smooth gray stone, and it got darker as we went, till I could no longer see the color of the floor, and the tiger seemed to absorb the whole of the daylight.

"A faint hope came to me from a story of a skeleton of a mouse, which had been found in a wall of a cathedral with the skeleton of a cat behind it. He had got where the cat could not follow, but it didn't do him much good. I hoped that, if ever I found such a refuge, the tiger would have more sense than that cat. But still the cave ran on, without getting as small as all that. Still the tiger wasn't hurrying, and that seemed to me to make the situation even more desperate. It seemed to show that the tiger was so sure. Of course I could smell him behind me, for he was still gaining; but the smell seemed almost too strong for a tiger nearly thirty yards behind, and the awful thought came to me that this cave which I hoped might shelter me was the tiger's own lair. That is very much what it seemed to me.

"Then came the hope, after going some distance, that the cave might soon come out through the little hill, though I don't know what good that would have done me. Still, absurd though it may seem, logically it seemed better to me to lose five yards in a hundred when walking in the open, if ever I could get there again, than what I was losing by going on all fours in a race with an animal to whom that sort of walking is natural. And then the uncertainties of the other side of the hill seemed better than those around me, as they often do in such cases, and I thought I might find a tree. But there was no draught in my face; there was only the smell of the tiger in the darkness, and I realized I should never come to the open air."

I glanced at the children's faces to see if Jorkens was holding their attention any better than I had done. They were certainly listening intently, though I could not see that they were showing much more interest than they had shown in my poor story. The idea came to me, which may have been quite unjust, that the sympathies of the girl, so far as she felt any, were on the side of the tiger. But that of course may only have been my fancy. I should perhaps say that it was in the autumn, and no lights had yet been turned on, and the room was growing dim. I repeat that it was no fault of mine: I had no idea what was coming.

"The tiger was gaining rapidly," Jorkens continued, "and the perfect smoothness of the limestone floor had made it quite clear by now that it must have for long been polished by soft feet, the large feet of a heavy animal: there was no roughness left on any edge upon which I had put my hand. And then the smooth floor came to a sheer smooth rock without crevice or crack in it, and no turn to the left or right. The cave had ended. I turned round in the dark and smelt, rather than saw, the tiger."

"What happened then?" asked one of the boys.

"He ate me," said Jorkens. "It is a ghost that is speaking to you."

And all the fuss that happened in that dim room was blamed entirely on me.

Obstinate Uncle Otis

Robert Arthur

My Uncle Otis was the most obstinate man in Vermont. If you know Vermonters, you know that means he was the most obstinate man in the world. It is nothing but the solemn truth to say that Uncle Otis was so obstinate he was more dangerous than the hydrogen bomb.

You find that hard to believe. Naturally. So I shall tell you just why Uncle Otis was dangerous—dangerous not only to all of mankind but to the solar system as well. Yes, and quite possibly to the entire universe.

His name was Morks, like mine—Otis Morks. He lived in Vermont and I had not seen him for some time. Then one morning I received an urgent telegram from my Aunt Edith, his sister. It said: OTIS STRUCK BY LIGHTNING. SITUATION SERIOUS. COME AT ONCE.

I left on the next train. Not only was I concerned for Uncle Otis, but there was an undertone of unexplained urgency in those ten commonplace words that compelled me to haste.

156

Late that afternoon I descended in Hillport, Vermont. The only taxi, an ancient sedan, was driven by a village character named Jud Perkins. Jud was also constable, and as I climbed into his decrepit vehicle I saw that he had a revolver strapped around his waist.

I also noticed, across the square, a knot of townspeople standing staring at something. Then I realized they were staring at an empty granite pedestal that had formerly held a large bronze statue to a local statesman named Ogilby—an individual Uncle Otis had always held in the utmost contempt.

Obstinately, Uncle Otis would never believe that anybody would erect a statue to Ogilby, and had always refused to admit that there actually was such a statue in the village square. But there had been, and now it was gone.

The old car lurched into motion. I leaned forward and asked Jud Perkins where the statue had gone. He turned to squint at me sideways.

"Stole," he informed me. "Yestiddy afternoon, about five. In plain view. Yessir, took between two winks of an eye. We was all in Simpkins' store—me 'n' Simpkins 'n' your Uncle Otis Morks 'n' your Aunt Edith 'n' some others. Somebody said as how the town ought to clean Ogilby's statue—become plumb pigeonfied last few years. Your Uncle Otis stuck out his chin.

"'What statue?' he wanted to know, his eyebrows bristlin'. 'There ain't no such thing as a statue to a blubbery-mouthed nincompoop like Ogilby in this town!'

"So, though I knowed it wasn't any use, he wouldn't believe in th' statue if he walked into it an' broke his leg— never met as obstinate a man as Otis Morks for not believing in a thing he don't like—anyway, I turned around to point at it. And it was gone. Minute before it had been there. Now it wasn't. Stole between one look an' th' next."

Jud Perkins spat out the window and turned to look at me

in an authoritative manner.

"If you want to know who done it," he said, "these here Fifth Columnists, that's who." (I should add that this occurred during World War II.) "They took Ogilby 'cause he's bronze, see? Over there, they need copper an' bronze for making shells. So they're stealin' it an' shippin' it over by submarine. But I got my eyes skinned for 'em if they come around here again. I got me my pistol an' I'm on th' watch."

We bumped and banged out toward Uncle Otis' farm, and Jud Perkins continued bringing me up to date on local affairs. He told me how Uncle Otis had come to be struck by lightning—out of his own obstinacy, as I had suspected.

"Day before yestidday," Jud told me, between expectorations of tobacco juice, "your Uncle Otis was out in th' fields when it blowed up a thunderstorm. He got in under a big oak tree. Told him myself a thousand times trees draw lightning, but he's too obstinate to listen.

"Maybe he thought he c'd ignore that lightning, like he ignores Willoughby's barn across the road, or Marble Hill, that his cousin Seth lawed away from him so that now he won't admit there is any such hill. Or th' new dam th' state put in to make a reservoir, and flooded some grazin' land he always used, so that now your Uncle Otis acts 's, if you're crazy when you talk about there bein' a dam there.

"Well, maybe he thought he c'd ignore that lightning, but lightning's hard to ignore. It hit that oak, splintered it an' knocked Otis twenty feet. Only reason it didn't kill him, I guess, is because he's always had such prime good health. Ain't been sick a day in his life except that week twenty years ago when he fell off a horse an' had his amnesia an' thought he was a farm machinery salesman named Eustace Lingham, from Cleveland, Ohio.

"Your Aunt Edith seen it happen and run out and drug him in. She put him to bed an' called Doc Perkins. Doc said it was just shock, he'd come to pretty soon, but keep him in bed two, three days.

"Sure enough, your Uncle Otis came to, 'bout supper, but he wouldn't stay in bed. Said he felt fine, and by dad, yestidday in Simpkins' store I never seen him lookin' more fit. Acted ten years younger. Walked like he was on springs an' seemed to give out electricity from every pore."

I asked if increasing age had softened Uncle Otis' natural obstinacy any. Jud spat with extra copiousness.

"Made it worse," he said flatly. "Most obstinate man in Vermont, your Uncle Otis. Dad blast it, when he says a thing ain't, even though it's right there in front of him, blamed if he don't say it so positive you almost believe him.

"Sat on his front stoop myself, only last week, with that old barn of Willoughby's spang in th' way of th' view, and your Uncle Otis lookin' at it 's if it weren't there.

"'Fine view,' I said, 'iffi'n only that barn warn't there,' an' your Uncle Otis looked at me like I was crazy.

"'Barn?' he said. 'What barn? No barn there an' never has been. Finest view in Vermont. See for twenty miles.'"

Jud Perkins chuckled and just missed running down a yellow dog and a boy on a bicycle.

"There's people got so much faith they can believe what ain't," he said. "But your Uncle Otis is th' only man I ever met so obstinate he c'n disbelieve in things that is."

I was in a thoughtful mood when Jud Perkins dropped me at Uncle Otis' gate. Uncle Otis wasn't in sight, but I headed around to the rear of the house and Aunt Edith came hurrying out of the kitchen, her apron, skirts, hair and hands all fluttering.

"Oh, Murchison!" she cried. "I'm so glad you're here. I don't know what to do, I simply don't. The most dreadful thing has happened to Otis, and—"

Then I saw Otis himself, going down the walk to get the evening paper from a tin receptacle at the gate. His small, spare figure upright and a stubborn jaw outthrust, his bushy white eyebrows bristling, he looked unaltered to me. But Aunt Edith only wrung her hands when I said so.

"I know," she sighed. "If you didn't know the truth, you'd think it actually did him good to be hit by lightning. But here he comes. I can't tell you any more now. After supper! He mustn't be allowed to guess—Oh, I do hope nothing dreadful happens before we can stop it."

And then, as Uncle Otis approached with his paper, she fled back into the kitchen.

Uncle Otis certainly did not seem changed, unless for the better. As Jud Perkins had remarked, he seemed younger. He shook my hand heartily and my arm tingled, as if from an electric shock. His eyes sparkled. His whole being seemed keyed up and buoyant with mysterious energy.

We strolled toward the front porch and stood facing the rotting old barn across the road that had spoiled the view. Grasping for a conversational topic as I studied Uncle Otis to discover what Aunt Edith meant, I suggested it was too bad the storm two days before hadn't blown the barn down and finished it.

"Barn?" Uncle Otis scowled at me. "What barn? No barn there, boy! Nothing but th' view—finest view in Vermont. If you c'n see a barn there you'd better get to a doctor fast as you can hike."

As Jud had said, he spoke so convincingly that in spite of myself I had to turn for another look at the structure. I remained staring for quite some time, I expect, and probably I blinked.

Because Uncle Otis was telling the truth.

There wasn't any barn—now.

All through supper a suspicion of the incredible truth grew on me. And after supper, while Uncle Otis read his paper in the parlor, I followed Aunt Edith into the kitchen.

She only sighed when I told her about the barn, and looked at me with haunted eyes.

"Yes," she whispered, "it's Otis. I knew when the statue. . .

went—yesterday when we were in Simpkins' store. I was looking right at it when Otis said what he did and it—it was just gone, right from under my eyes. That's when I sent you the telegram."

"You mean," I asked, "that since Uncle Otis was struck by lightning, his obstinacy has taken a new turn? He used to think things he didn't like didn't exist, and that was all. But now, when he thinks it, due to some peculiar heightening of his tremendously obstinate will power, the things *don't* exist? He just disbelieves them right out of existence?"

Aunt Edith nodded. "They just *go!*" she cried, almost wildly. "When he says a thing's not, now it's *not*."

I confess the idea made me uneasy. There were a number of unpleasant possibilities that occurred to me. The list of things—and people—Uncle Otis didn't believe in was long and varied.

"What," I asked, "do you suppose the limit is? A statue, a barn—where do you suppose it stops?"

"I don't know," she told me. "Maybe there isn't any limit to it. Otis is an *awfully* obstinate man and—well, suppose something reminds him about the dam? Suppose he says there isn't any dam? It's a hundred feet high and all that water behind it—"

She did not have to finish. If Uncle Otis suddenly disbelieved the Hillport dam out of existence, the impounded water that would be set free would wipe away the village, and might kill the whole five hundred inhabitants.

"And then, of course, there are all those far-off countries with the funny names he's never believed were real," Aunt Edith whispered. "Like Zanzibar and Martinique."

"And Guatemala and Polynesia," I agreed, frowning. "If he were reminded of one of those by something, and took it into his head to declare it didn't exist, there's no telling what might happen. The sudden disappearance of any one of them—why, tidal waves and earthquakes would be the least we could expect."

"But what can we do to stop him?" Aunt Edith wanted to know, desperately. "We can't tell him that he mustn't—"

She was interrupted by a snort as Uncle Otis marched into the kitchen with the evening paper.

"Listen to this!" he commanded, and read us a short item, the gist of which was that Seth Youngman, the second cousin who had lawsuited his hill away from him, was planning to sell Marble Hill to a New York company that would quarry it. Then Uncle Otis threw the paper down on the kitchen table in disgust.

"What they talking about?" he barked, his eyebrows bristling. "Marble Hill? No hill around here by that name, and never has been. And Seth Youngman never owned a hill in his life. What kind of idiots get this paper out, I want to know?"

He glowered at us. And in the silence, a faint distant rumbling, as of displaced stones, could be heard. Aunt Edith and I turned as one. It was still light, and from the kitchen window we could see to the northwest, where Marble Hill stood up against the horizon like a battered derby hat—or where it *had* stood.

The ancient prophets may have had faith strong enough to move mountains. But Uncle Otis was possessed of something far more remarkable, it seemed—a lack of faith which could unmove them.

Uncle Otis himself, unaware of anything unusual, picked up the paper again, grumbling.

"Everybody's crazy these days," he declared. "Piece here about President Roosevelt. Not Teddy Roosevelt, but somebody called Franklin. Can't even get a man's name straight. Everybody ought to know there's no such president as Franklin Roo—"

"Uncle Otis!" I shouted. "Look, there's a mouse!"

Uncle Otis stopped and turned. There *was* a mouse,

crouched under the stove, and it was the only thing I could
think of to distract Uncle Otis' attention before he expressed
his disbelief in Franklin D. Roosevelt. I was barely in time.
I dabbed at my brow. Uncle Otis scowled.

"Where?" he demanded. "No mouse there I can see."

"Th—" I started to point. Then I checked myself. As soon
as he had spoken, of course, the mouse was gone. I said instead that I must have been mistaken. Uncle Otis snorted and
strode back toward the parlor. Aunt Edith and I looked at
each other.

"If he'd said—" she began. "—if he'd finished saying there
isn't any President Roose—"

She never completed the sentence. Uncle Otis, going through
the doorway, caught his foot in a hole worn through the
linoleum and fell full length into the hall. As he went down,
his head struck a table, and he was unconscious when we
reached him.

I carried Uncle Otis into the parlor and laid him on the
old horsehair sofa. Aunt Edith brought a cold compress and
spirits of ammonia. Together we worked over Uncle Otis'
limp form, and presently he opened his eyes, blinking at us
without recognition.

"Who're you?" he demanded. "What happened to me?"

"Otis!" Aunt Edith cried. "I'm your sister. You fell and hit
your head. You've been unconscious."

Uncle Otis glowered at us with deep suspicion. "Otis?" he
repeated. "My name's not Otis. Who you think I am, anyway?"

"But it *is* Otis!" Aunt Edith wailed. "You're Otis Morks,
my brother, and you live in Hillport, Vermont. You've lived
here all your life."

Uncle Otis' lower lip stuck out obstinately.

"My name's *not* Otis Morks," he declared, rising. "I'm
Eustace Lingham, of Cleveland, Ohio. I sell farm machinery.
I'm not your brother. I've never seen you before, either of
you. I've got a headache and I'm tired of talking. I'm going

out and get some fresh air. Maybe it'll make my head feel better."

Dumbly Aunt Edith stood to one side. Uncle Otis marched out into the hall and through the front door. Aunt Edith, peering out the window, reported that he was standing on the front steps, looking up at the stars.

"It's happened again," she said despairingly. "His amnesia's come back. Just like the time twenty years ago when he fell off a horse and thought he was this Eustace Lingham from Cleveland for a whole week.

"Oh, Murchison, now we've got to call the doctor. But if the doctor finds out about the other, he'll want to shut him up. Only, if anybody tries to shut Otis up, he'll just disbelieve in them and the place they want to shut him up in, too. Then they—they—"

"But if something isn't done," I pointed out, "there's no telling what may happen. He's bound to read about President Roosevelt again. You can't miss his name in the papers these days, even in Vermont. Or else he'll come across a mention of Madagascar or Guatemala."

"Or get into a fuss with the income tax people," Aunt Edith put in. "He keeps getting letters from them about why he's never paid any income tax. The last letter, they said they were going to send somebody to call on him in person. But he says there isn't any such thing as an income tax, so there can't be any income-tax collectors. So if a man comes here saying he's an income-tax collector, Uncle Otis will just not believe in him. Then. . ."

Helplessly we looked at each other. Aunt Edith grabbed my arm.

"Murchison!" she gasped. "Quick! Go out with him. We mustn't leave him alone. Only last week he decided that there aren't any such things as stars!"

I did not hesitate an instant. A moment later I was on the porch beside Uncle Otis, who was breathing in the cool evening air and staring upward at the spangled heavens, a look of deepest disbelief on his face.

"Stars!" he barked, stabbing a skinny forefinger toward the star-dotted sky. "A hundred million billion trillion dillion miles away, every last one of 'em! And every one of 'em a hundred times bigger 'n the sun! That's what the book said. You know what *I* say? I say bah! Nothing's that big, or that far off. You know what those things they look at through telescopes and call stars are? They're not stars at all. Fact is, there's no such thing as st—"

"Uncle Otis!" I cried loudly. "A mosquito!"

And I brought my hand down on the top of his head with solid force.

I had to distract him. I had to keep him from saying it. The universe is a big thing, of course, probably too big even for Uncle Otis to disbelieve out of existence. But I didn't dare take a chance. So I yelled and slapped him.

But I'd forgotten about the return of his ancient amnesia, and his belief that he was Eustace Lingham of Cleveland. When he had recovered from my blow he stared at me coldly.

"I'm not your Uncle Otis!" he snapped. "I'm nobody's Uncle Otis. I'm nobody's brother, either. I'm Eustace Lingham and I've got a headache. I'm going to have my cigar and I'm going to bed, and in the morning I'm going back to Cleveland."

He turned, stamped inside, and went up the stairs.

I trailed after him, unable to think of a helpful plan, and Aunt Edith followed us both up the stairs. She and I came to a stop at the top. Together we watched Uncle Otis stride into his room and close the door.

After that we heard the bedsprings squeak as he sat down. This was followed by the scratching of a match and in a moment we smelled cigar smoke. Uncle Otis always allowed himself one cigar, just before going to bed.

"Otis Morks!" we heard him mutter to himself, and one shoe dropped to the floor. "Nobody's got such a name. It's a trick of some kind. Don't believe there is any such person."

Then he was silent. The silence continued. We waited for him to drop the other shoe . . . and when a full minute had passed, we gave each other one horrified look, rushed to the door and threw it open.

Aunt Edith and I stared in. The window was closed and locked. A cigar in an ash tray on a table by the bed was sending a feather of smoke upwards. There was a hollow in the bed covers, slowly smoothing out, where someone might have been sitting a moment before. A single one of Uncle Otis' shoes lay on the floor beside the bed.

But Uncle Otis, of course, was gone. He had disbelieved himself out of existence. . . .

The Waxwork

A. M. Burrage

While the uniformed attendants of Marriner's Waxworks were ushering the last stragglers through the great glass-paneled double doors, the manager sat in his office interviewing Raymond Hewson.

The manager was a youngish man, stout, blond and of medium height. He wore his clothes well and contrived to look extremely smart without appearing over-dressed. Raymond Hewson looked neither. His clothes, which had been good when new and which were still carefully brushed and pressed, were beginning to show signs of their owner's losing battle with the world. He was a small, spare, pale man, with lank, errant brown hair, and although he spoke plausibly and even forcibly he had the defensive and somewhat furtive air of a man who was used to rebuffs. He looked what he was, a man gifted somewhat above the ordinary, who was a failure through his lack of self-assertion.

The manager was speaking.

"There is nothing new in your request," he said. "In fact

we refuse it to different people—mostly young bloods who have tried to make bets—about three times a week. We have nothing to gain and something to lose by letting people spend the night in our Murderers' Den. If I allowed it, and some young idiot lost his senses, what would be my position? But your being a journalist somewhat alters the case."

Hewson smiled.

"I suppose you mean that journalists have no senses to lose."

"No, no," laughed the manager, "but one imagines them to be responsible people. Besides, here we have something to gain; publicity and advertisement."

"Exactly," said Hewson, "and there I thought we might come to terms."

The manager laughed again.

"Oh," he exclaimed, "I know what's coming. You want to be paid twice, do you? It used to be said years ago that Madame Tussaud's would give a man a hundred pounds for sleeping alone in the Chamber of Horrors. I hope you don't think that we have made any such offer. Er—what is your paper, Mr. Hewson?"

"I am free-lancing at present," Hewson confessed, "working on space for several papers. However, I should find no difficulty in getting the story printed. The *Morning Echo* would use it like a shot. 'A Night with Marriner's Murderers.' No live paper could turn it down."

The manager rubbed his chin.

"Ah! And how do you propose to treat it?"

"I shall make it gruesome, of course; gruesome with just a saving touch of humor."

The other nodded and offered Hewson his cigarette case.

"Very well, Mr. Hewson," he said. "Get your story printed in the *Morning Echo,* and there will be a five-pound note waiting for you here when you care to come and call for it.

But first of all, it's no small ordeal that you're proposing to undertake. I'd like to be quite sure about you, and I'd like you to be quite sure about yourself. I own I shouldn't care to take it on. I've seen those figures dressed and undressed. I know all about the process of their manufacture. I can walk about in company downstairs as unmoved as if I were walking among so many skittles. But I should hate having to sleep down there alone among them."

"Why?" asked Hewson.

"I don't know. There isn't any reason. I don't believe in ghosts. If I did I should expect them to haunt the scene of their crimes or the spot where their bodies were laid, instead of a cellar which happens to contain their waxwork effigies. It's just that I couldn't sit alone among them all night, with their seeming to stare at me in the way they do. After all, they represent the lowest and most appalling types of humanity, and—although I would not own it publicly—the people who come to see them are not generally charged with the very highest motives. The whole atmosphere of the place is unpleasant, and if you are susceptible to atmosphere I warn you that you are in for a very uncomfortable night."

Hewson had known that from the moment when the idea had first occurred to him. His soul sickened at the prospect, even while he smiled casually upon the manager. But he had a wife and family to keep, and for the past month he had been living on paragraphs, eked out by his rapidly dwindling store of savings. Here was a chance not to be missed—the price of a special story in the *Morning Echo,* with a five-pound note to add to it. It meant comparative wealth and luxury for a week, and freedom from the worst anxieties for a fortnight. Besides, if he wrote the story well, it might lead to an offer of regular employment.

"The way of transgressors—and newspaper men—is hard," he said. "I have already promised myself an uncomfortable night because your murderers' den is obviously not fitted up as a hotel bedroom. But I don't think your waxworks will worry me much."

"You're not superstitious?"

"Not a bit." Hewson laughed.

"But you're a journalist; you must have a strong imagination."

"The news editors for whom I've worked have always complained that I haven't any. Plain facts are not considered sufficient in our trade, and the papers don't like offering their readers unbuttered bread."

The manager smiled and rose.

"Right," he said. "I think the last of the people have gone. Wait a moment. I'll give orders for the figures downstairs not to be draped, and let the night people know that you'll be here. Then I'll take you down and show you round."

He picked up the receiver of a house telephone, spoke into it and presently replaced it.

"One condition I'm afraid I must impose on you," he remarked. "I must ask you not to smoke. We had a fire scare down in the Murderers' Den this evening. I don't know who gave the alarm, but whoever it was it was a false one. Fortunately there were very few people down there at the time, or there might have been a panic. And now, if you're ready, we'll make a move."

Hewson followed the manager through half a dozen rooms where attendants were busy shrouding the kings and queens of England, the generals and prominent statesmen of this and other generations, all the mixed herd of humanity whose fame or notoriety had rendered them eligible for this kind of immortality. The manager stopped once and spoke to a man in uniform, saying something about an armchair in the Murderers' Den.

"It's the best we can do for you, I'm afraid," he said to Hewson. "I hope you'll be able to get some sleep."

He led the way through an open barrier and down ill-lit stone stairs which conveyed a sinister impression of giving access to a dungeon. In a passage at the bottom were a few preliminary horrors, such as relics of the Inquisition, a rack taken from a mediæval castle, branding irons, thumbscrews, and other mementoes of man's one-time cruelty to man. Beyond the passage was the Murderers' Den.

It was a room of irregular shape with a vaulted roof, and dimly lit by electric lights burning behind inverted bowls of frosted glass. It was, by design, an eerie and uncomfortable chamber—a chamber whose atmosphere invited its visitors to speak in whispers. There was something of the air of a chapel about it, but a chapel no longer devoted to the practice of piety and given over now for base and impious worship.

The waxwork murderers stood on low pedestals with numbered tickets at their feet. Seeing them elsewhere, and without knowing whom they represented, one would have thought them a dull-looking crew, chiefly remarkable for the shabbiness of their clothes.

Recent notorieties rubbed dusty shoulders with the old "favorites." Thurtell, the murderer of Weir, stood as if frozen in the act of making a shop-window gesture to young Bywaters. There was Lefroy, the poor half-baked little snob who killed for gain so that he might ape the gentleman. Charles Peace, the only member of that vile company who looked uncompromisingly and entirely evil, sneered across a gangway at Norman Thorne.

The manager, walking around with Hewson, pointed out several of the more interesting of these unholy notabilities.

"That's Crippen; I expect you recognize him. Insignificant little beast who looks as if he couldn't tread on a worm. That's Armstrong. Looks like a decent, harmless country gentleman, doesn't he? There's old Vaquier; you can't miss him because of his beard. And of course this—"

"Who's that?" Hewson interrupted in a whisper, pointing.

"Oh, I was coming to him," said the manager in a light undertone. "Come and have a good look at him. This is our star turn. He's the only one of the bunch that hasn't been hanged."

The figure which Hewson had indicated was that of a small, slight man not much more than five feet in height. It wore little waxed moustaches, large spectacles, and a caped coat. There was something so exaggeratedly French in its appearance that it reminded Hewson of a stage caricature. He could not have said precisely why the mild-looking face seemed to him so repellent, but he had already recoiled a step and, even in the manager's company, it cost him an effort to look again.

"But who is he?" he asked.

"That," said the manager, "is Dr. Bourdette."

Hewson shook his head doubtfully.

"I think I've heard the name," he said, "but I forget in connection with what."

The manager smiled.

"You'd remember better if you were a Frenchman," he said. "For some long while that man was the terror of Paris. He carried on his work of healing by day, and of throat-cutting by night, when the fit was on him. He killed for the sheer devilish pleasure it gave him to kill, and always in the same way—with a razor. After his last crime he left a clue behind him which set the police upon his track. One clue led to another, and before very long they knew that they were on the track of the Parisian equivalent of our Jack the Ripper, and had enough evidence to send him to the madhouse or the guillotine on a dozen capital charges.

"But even then our friend here was too clever for them. When he realized that the toils were closing about him he mysteriously disappeared, and ever since the police of every civilized country have been looking for him. There is no doubt that he managed to make away with himself, and by some means which has prevented his body coming to light. One or two crimes of a similar nature have taken place since his disappearance, but he is believed almost for certain to be dead. It's queer, isn't it, how every notorious murderer has imitators?"

Hewson shuddered and fidgeted with his feet.

"I don't like him at all," he confessed. "Ugh! What eyes he's got!"

"Yes, this figure's a little masterpiece. You find the eyes bite into you? Well, that's excellent realism, then, for Bourdette practised mesmerism, and was supposed to mesmerize his victims before dispatching them. Indeed, had he not done so, it is impossible to see how so small a man could have done his ghastly work. There were never any signs of a struggle."

"I thought I saw him move," said Hewson with a catch in his voice.

The manager smiled.

"You'll have more than one optical illusion before the night's out, I expect. You shan't be locked in. You can come upstairs when you've had enough of it. There are watchmen on the premises, so you'll find company. Don't be alarmed if you hear them moving about. I'm sorry I can't give you any more light, because all the lights are on. For obvious reasons we keep this place as gloomy as possible."

The member of the night staff who placed the armchair for Hewson was inclined to be facetious.

"Where will you have it, sir?" he asked, grinning. "Just 'ere, so as you can 'ave a little talk with Crippen when you're tired of sitting still? Say where, sir."

Hewson smiled. The man's chaff pleased him if only because, for the moment at least, it lent the proceedings a much-desired air of the commonplace.

"I'll place it myself, thanks," he said. "I'll find out where the draughts come from first."

"You won't find any down here. Well, good night, sir. I'm

upstairs if you want me. Don't let 'em sneak up be'ind you
and touch your neck with their cold and clammy 'ands."

Hewson laughed and wished the man good night. It was
easier than he had expected. He wheeled the armchair—a
heavy one upholstered in plush—a little way down the central
gangway, and deliberately turned it so that its back was towards the effigy of Dr. Bourdette. For some undefined reason
he liked Dr. Bourdette a great deal less than his companions.
Busying himself with arranging the chair he was almost light-
hearted, but when the attendant's footfalls had died away and
a deep hush stole over the chamber he realized that he had
no slight ordeal before him.

The dim unwavering light fell on the rows of figures which
were so uncannily like human beings that the silence and the
stillness seemed unnatural and even ghastly. He missed the
sound of breathing, the rustling of clothes, the hundred and
one minute noises one hears when even the deepest silence
has fallen upon a crowd. But the air was as stagnant as
water at the bottom of a standing pond. There was not a
breath in the chamber to stir a curtain or rustle a hanging
drapery or start a shadow. His own shadow, moving in re-
sponse to a shifted arm or leg, was all that could be coaxed
into motion. All was still to the gaze and silent to the ear.
"It must be like this at the bottom of the sea," he thought,
and wondered how to work the phrase into his story on the
morrow.

He faced the sinister figures boldly enough. They were only
waxworks. So long as he let that thought dominate all others
he promised himself that all would be well. It did not, however, save him long from the discomfort occasioned by the
waxen stare of Dr. Bourdette, which, he knew, was directed
upon him from behind. The eyes of the little Frenchman's
effigy haunted and tormented him, and he itched with the desire to turn and look.

"Come!" he thought, "my nerves have started already. If I

turn and look at that dressed-up dummy it will be an admission of funk."

And then another voice in his brain spoke to him.

"It's because you're afraid that you won't turn and look at him."

The two Voices quarreled silently for a moment or two, and at last Hewson slewed his chair round a little and looked behind him.

Among the many figures standing in stiff, unnatural poses, the effigy of the dreadful little doctor stood out with a queer prominence, perhaps because a steady beam of light beat straight down upon it. Hewson flinched before the parody of mildness which some fiendishly skilled craftsman had managed to convey in wax, met the eyes for one agonized second, and turned again to face the other direction.

"He's only a waxwork like the rest of you," Hewson muttered defiantly. "You're all only waxworks."

They were only waxworks, yes, but waxworks don't move. Not that he had seen the least movement anywhere, but it struck him that, in the moment or two while he had looked behind him, there had been the least subtle change in the grouping of the figures in front. Crippen, for instance, seemed to have turned at least one degree to the left. Or, thought Hewson, perhaps the illusion was due to the fact that he had not slewed his chair back into its exact original position. Hewson held his breath for a moment, and then drew his courage back to him as a man lifts a weight. He remembered the words of more than one news editor and laughed savagely to himself.

"And they tell me I've got no imagination!" he said beneath his breath.

He took a notebook from his pocket and wrote quickly.

"Mem.—Deathly silence and unearthly stillness of figures. Like being bottom of sea. Hypnotic eyes of Dr. Bourdette. Figures seem to move when not being watched."

He closed the book suddenly over his fingers and looked round quickly and awfully over his right shoulder. He had neither seen nor heard a movement, but it was as if some sixth sense had made him aware of one. He looked straight into the vapid countenance of Lefroy which smiled back as if to say, "It wasn't I!"

Of course it wasn't he, or any of them; it was his own nerves. Or was it? Hadn't Crippen moved again during that moment when his attention was directed elsewhere? You couldn't trust that little man! Once you took your eyes off him he took advantage of it to shift his position. That was what they were all doing, if he only knew it, he told himself; and half rose out of his chair. This was not quite good enough! He was going. He wasn't going to spend the night with a lot of waxworks which moved while he wasn't looking.

. . . 'Hewson sat down again. This was very cowardly and very absurd. They *were* only waxworks and they *couldn't* move; let him hold that thought and all would yet be well. Then why all that silent unrest about him?—a subtle something in the air which did not quite break the silence and happened, whichever way he looked, just beyond the boundaries of his vision.

He swung round quickly to encounter the mild but baleful stare of Dr. Bourdette. Then, without warning, he jerked his head back to stare straight at Crippen. Ha! he'd nearly caught Crippen that time! "You'd better be careful, Crippen— and all the rest of you! If I do see one of you move I'll smash you to pieces! Do you hear?"

He ought to go, he told himself. Already he had experienced enough to write his story, or ten stories, for that matter. Well, then, why not go? The *Morning Echo* would be none the wiser as to how long he had stayed, nor would it care so long as his story was a good one. Yes, but that night watchman upstairs would chaff him. And the manager—one never knew—perhaps the manager would quibble over that five-pound note which he needed so badly. He wondered if Rose were asleep or if she were lying awake and thinking of him. She'd laugh when he told her that he had imagined . . .

This was a little too much! It was bad enough that the waxwork effigies of murderers should move when they weren't being watched, but it was intolerable that they should *breathe*. Somebody was breathing. Or was it his own breath which sounded to him as if it came from a distance? He sat rigid, listening and straining until he exhaled with a long sigh. His own breath after all, or—if not, Something had divined that he was listening and had ceased breathing simultaneously.

Hewson jerked his head swiftly around and looked all about him out of haggard and hunted eyes. Everywhere his gaze encountered the vacant waxen faces, and everywhere he felt that by just some least fraction of a second he had missed seeing a movement of hand or foot, a silent opening or compression of lips, a flicker of eyelids, a look of human intelligence now smoothed out. They were like naughty children in a class, whispering, fidgeting and laughing behind their teacher's back, but blandly innocent when his gaze was turned upon them.

This would not do! This distinctly would not do! He must clutch at something, grip with his mind upon something which belonged essentially to the workaday world, to the daylight London streets. He was Raymond Hewson, an unsuccessful journalist, a living and breathing man, and these figures grouped around him were only dummies, so they could neither move nor whisper. What did it matter if they were supposed to be lifelike effigies of murderers? They were only made of wax and sawdust, and stood there for the entertainment of morbid sightseers and orange-sucking trippers. That was better! Now what was that funny story which somebody had told him yesterday? . . .

He recalled part of it, but not all, for the gaze of Dr.

Bourdette urged, challenged, and finally compelled him to turn.

Hewson half-turned, and then swung his chair so as to bring him face to face with the wearer of those dreadful hypnotic eyes. His own eyes were dilated, and his mouth, at first set in a grin of terror, lifted at the corners in a snarl. Then Hewson spoke and woke a hundred sinister echoes.

"You moved, blast you!" he cried. "Yes, you did, blast you! I saw you!"

Then he sat quite still, staring straight before him, like a man found frozen in the Arctic snows.

Dr. Bourdette's movements were leisurely. He stepped off his pedestal with the mincing care of a lady alighting from a bus. The platform stood about two feet from the ground, and above the edge of it a plush-covered rope hung in arc-like curves. Dr. Bourdette lifted up the rope until it formed an arch for him to pass under, stepped off the platform and sat down on the edge facing Hewson. Then he nodded and smiled and said, "Good evening."

"I need hardly tell you," he continued, in perfect English in which was traceable only the least foreign accent, "that not until I overheard the conversation between you and the worthy manager of this establishment did I suspect that I should have the pleasure of a companion here for the night. You cannot move or speak without my bidding, but you can hear me perfectly well. Something tells me that you are—shall I say nervous? My dear sir, have no illusions. I am not one of these contemptible effigies miraculously come to life: I am Dr. Bourdette himself."

He paused, coughed, and shifted his legs.

"Pardon me," he resumed, "but I am a little stiff. And let me explain. Circumstances with which I need not fatigue you have made it desirable that I should live in England. I was close to this building this evening when I saw a policeman regarding me a thought too curiously. I guessed that he intended to follow and perhaps ask me embarrassing questions, so I mingled with the crowd and came in here. An extra coin bought my admission to the chamber in which we now meet, and an inspiration showed me a certain means of escape.

"I raised a cry of fire, and when all the fools had rushed to the stairs I stripped my effigy of the caped coat which you behold me wearing, donned it, hid my effigy under the platform at the back, and took its place on the pedestal.

"I own that I have since spent a very fatiguing evening, but fortunately I was not always being watched and had opportunities to draw an occasional deep breath and ease the rigidity of my pose. One small boy screamed and exclaimed that he saw me moving. I understood that he was to be whipped and put straight to bed on his return home.

"The manager's description of me, which I had the embarrassment of being compelled to overhear, was biased but not altogether inaccurate. Clearly I am not dead, although it is as well that the world thinks otherwise. His account of my hobby, which I have indulged for years, was in the main true although not intelligently expressed. The world is divided between collectors and non-collectors. With the non-collectors we are not concerned. The collectors collect anything, according to their individual tastes, from money to cigarette cards, from moths to matchboxes. I collect throats."

He paused again and regarded Hewson's throat with interest mingled with disfavor.

"I am obliged to the chance which brought us together tonight," he continued, "and perhaps it would seem ungrateful to complain. From motives of personal safety my activities have been somewhat curtailed of late years, and I am glad of this opportunity of gratifying my somewhat unusual whim. But you have a skinny neck, sir, if you will overlook a personal remark. I should never have selected you from choice. I like men with thick necks . . . thick red necks . . ."

He fumbled in an inside pocket and took out something which he tested against a wet forefinger and then proceeded to pass gently to and fro across the palm of his left hand.

"This is a little French razor," he remarked blandly. "They are not much used in England, but perhaps you know them? One strops them on wood. The blade, you will observe, is very narrow. They do not cut very deep, but deep enough. In just one little moment you shall see for yourself. I shall ask you the little civil question of all the polite barbers: Does the razor suit you, sir?"

He rose up, a diminutive but menacing figure of evil, and approached Hewson with the silent, furtive step of a hunting panther.

"You will have the goodness," he said, "to raise your chin a little. Thank you, and a little more. Just a little more. Ah, thank you! . . . *Merci, m'sieur . . . Ah, merci . . . merci. . . .*"

Over one end of the chamber was a thick skylight of frosted glass which, by day, let in a few sickly and filtered rays from the floor above. After sunrise these began to mingle with the subdued light from the electric bulbs, and this mingled illumination added a certain ghastliness to a scene which needed no additional touch of horror.

The waxwork figures stood apathetically in their places, waiting to be admired or execrated by the crowds who would presently wander fearfully among them. In their midst, Hewson sat still, leaning far back in his armchair. His chin was uptilted as if he were waiting to receive attention from a barber, and although there was not a scratch upon his throat, nor anywhere upon his body, he was cold and dead. His previous employers were wrong in having him credited with no imagination.

Dr. Bourdette on his pedestal watched the dead man unemotionally. He did not move, nor was he capable of motion. But then, after all, he was only a waxwork.

The Isle of Voices

Robert Louis Stevenson

Keola was married with Lehua, daughter of Kalamake, the
wise man of Molokai, and he kept his dwelling with the
father of his wife. There was no man more cunning than that
prophet. He read the stars, he could divine by the bodies of
the dead, and by the means of evil creatures: he could go
alone into the highest parts of the mountain, into the region
of the hobgoblins, and there he would lay snares to entrap
the spirits of ancient.

For this reason no man was more consulted in all the
Kingdom of Hawaii. Prudent people bought, and sold, and
married, and laid out their lives by his counsels; and the
King had him twice to Kona to seek the treasures of Kamehameha. Neither was any man more feared. Of his enemies,
some had dwindled in sickness by the virtue of his incanta-
tions, and some had been spirited away, so that folk looked
in vain for so much as a bone of their bodies. It was
rumored that he had the art or the gift of the old heroes.

182

Men had seen him at night upon the mountains, stepping from one cliff to the next. They had seen him walking in the high forest, and his head and shoulders were above the trees.

This Kalamake was a strange man to see. He was come of the best blood in Molokai and Maui, of a pure descent; and yet he was more white to look upon than any foreigner; his hair the color of dry grass, and his eyes red and very blind, so that "Blind as Kalamake that can see across to-morrow," was a by-word in the islands.

Of all these doings of his father-in-law, Keola knew a little by the common repute, a little more he suspected, and the rest he ignored. But there was one thing troubled him. Kalamake was a man who spared for nothing, whether to eat or to drink or to wear; and for all he paid in bright new dollars. "Bright as Kalamake's dollars," was another saying in the Eight Isles. Yet he neither sold, nor planted, nor took hire—only now and then from his sorceries—and there was no source conceivable for so much silver coin.

It chanced one day Keola's wife was gone upon a visit to Kaunakakai on the lee side of the island, and the men were forth at the sea-fishing. But Keola was an idle dog, and he lay in the veranda and watched the surf beat on the shore and the birds fly about the cliff. It was a chief thought with him always—the thought of the bright dollars. When he lay down to bed he would be wondering why they were so many, and when he woke at morn he would be wondering why they were all new; and the thing was never absent from his mind. But this day of all days he made sure in his heart of some discovery. For it seems he had observed the place where Kalamake kept his treasure, which was a lock-fast desk against the parlor wall, under the print of Kamehameha the fifth, and a photograph of Queen Victoria with her crown. And it seems again that, no later than the night before, he found occasion to look in, and behold! the bag lay there empty. And this was the day of the steamer; he could see her smoke off Kalaupapa; and she must soon arrive with a month's goods, tinned salmon and gin, and all manner of rare luxuries for Kalamake.

"Now if he can pay for his goods today," Keola thought, "I shall know for certain that the man is a warlock, and the dollars come out of the Devil's pocket."

While he was so thinking, there was his father-in-law behind him, looking vexed.

"Is that the steamer?" he asked.

"Yes," said Keola. "She has but to call at Pelekunu, and then she will be here."

"There is no help for it then," returned Kalamake, "and I must take you into my confidence, Keola, for the lack of anyone better. Come here within the house."

So they stepped together into the parlor, which was a very fine room, papered and hung with prints, and furnished with a rocking chair, and a table and a sofa in the European style. There was a shelf of books besides, and a family Bible in the midst of the table, and the lock-fast writing-desk against the wall; so that anyone could see it was the house of a man of substance.

Kalamake made Keola close the shutters of the windows, while he himself locked all the doors and set open the lid of the desk. From this he brought forth a pair of necklaces hung with charms and shells, a bundle of dried herbs, and the dried leaves of trees, and a green branch of palm.

"What I am about," said he, "is a thing beyond wonder. The men of old were wise; they wrought marvels, and this among the rest; but that was at night in the dark, under the fit stars and in the desert. The same will I do here in my own house, and under the plain eye of day."

So saying, he put the Bible under the cushion of the sofa so that it was all covered, brought out from the same place a mat of a wonderfully fine texture, and heaped the herbs and leaves on sand in a tin pan. And then he and Keola put on the necklaces, and took their stand upon the opposite corners of the mat.

"The time comes," said the warlock; "be not afraid."

With that he set flame to the herbs, and began to mutter and wave the branch of palm. At first the light was dim because of the closed shutters; but the herbs caught strongly afire, and the flames beat upon Keola, and the room glowed with the burning; and next the smoke rose and made his head swim and his eyes darken, and the sound of Kalamake muttering ran in his ears. And suddenly, to the mat on which they were standing came a snatch or twitch, that seemed to be more swift than lightning. In the same wink the room was gone, and the house, the breath all beaten from Keola's body. Volumes of sun rolled upon his eyes and head, and he found himself transported to a beach of the sea, under a strong sun, with a great surf roaring: he and the warlock standing there on the same mat, speechless, gasping and grasping at one another, and passing their hands before their eyes.

"What was this?" cried Keola, who came to himself the first, because he was the younger. "The pang of it was like death."

"It matters not," panted Kalamake. "It is now done."

"And, in the name of God, where are we?" cried Keola.

"That is not the question," replied the sorcerer. "Being here, we have matter in our hands, and that we must attend to. Go, while I recover my breath, into the borders of the wood, and bring me the leaves of such and such an herb, and such and such a tree, which you will find to grow there plentifully—three handfuls of each and be speedy. We must be home again before the steamer comes; it would seem strange if we had disappeared." And he sat on the sand and panted.

Keola went up the beach, which was of shining sand and coral, strewn with singular shells; and he thought in his heart:

"How do I know this beach? I will come here again and gather shells."

In front of him was a line of palms against the sky; not like the palms of the Eight Islands, but tall and fresh and beautiful, and hanging out withered fans like gold among the green, and he thought in his heart:

"It is strange I should not have found this grove. I will come here again, when it is warm, to sleep." And he thought, "How warm it has grown suddenly!" For it was winter in Hawaii, and the day had been chill. And he thought also, "Where are the gray mountains? And where is the high cliff with the hanging forest and the wheeling birds?" And the more he considered, the less he might conceive in what quarter of the islands he was fallen.

In the border of the grove, where it met the beach, the herb was growing, but the tree farther back. Now, as Keola went toward the tree, he was aware of a young woman who had nothing on her body but a belt of leaves.

"Well!" thought Keola, "they are not very particular about their dress in this part of the country." And he paused, supposing she would observe him and escape; and seeing that she still looked before her, stood and hummed aloud. Up she leaped at the sound. Her face was ashen; she looked this way and that, and her mouth gaped with the terror of her soul. But it was a strange thing that her eyes did not rest upon Keola.

"Good day," said he. "You need not be so frightened, I will not eat you." And he had scarce opened his mouth before the young woman fled into the bush.

"These are strange manners," thought Keola, and, not thinking what he did, ran after her.

As he ran, the girl kept crying in some speech that was not

practiced in Hawaii, yet some of the words were the same, and he knew she kept calling and warning others. And presently he saw more people running—men, women, and children, one with another, all running and crying like people at a fire. And with that he began to grow afraid himself, and returned to Kalamake bringing the leaves. Him he told what he had seen.

"You must pay no heed," said Kalamake. "All this is like a dream and shadows. All will disappear and be forgotten."

"It seemed none saw me," said Keola.

"And none did," replied the sorcerer. "We walk here in the broad sun invisible by reason of these charms. Yet they hear us; and therefore it is well to speak softly, as I do."

With that he made a circle round the mat with stones, and in the midst he set the leaves.

"It will be your part," said he, "to keep the leaves alight, and feed the fire slowly. While they blaze (which is but for a little moment) I must do my errand; and before the ashes blacken, the same power that brought us carries us away. Be ready now with the match; and do you call me in good time lest the flames burn out and I be left."

As soon as the leaves caught, the sorcerer leaped like a deer out of the circle, and began to race along the beach like a hound that has been bathing. As he ran, he kept stooping to snatch shells; and it seemed to Keola that they glittered as he took them. The leaves blazed with a clear flame that consumed them swiftly; and presently Keola had but a handful left, and the sorcerer was far off, running and stopping.

"Back!" cried Keola. "Back! The leaves are near done."

At that Kalamake turned, and if he had run before, now he flew. But fast as he ran, the leaves burned faster. The flame was ready to expire when, with a great leap, he bounded on the mat. The wind of his leaping blew it out; and with that the beach was gone, and the sun and the sea; and they stood once more in the dimness of the shuttered parlor, and were once more shaken and blinded; and on the mat betwixt them lay a pile of shining dollars. Keola ran to the shutters; and there was the steamer tossing in the swell close in.

The same night Kalamake took his son-in-law apart, and gave him five dollars in his hand.

"Keola," said he, "if you are a wise man (which I am doubtful of) you will think you slept this afternoon on the veranda, and dreamed as you were sleeping. I am a man of few words, and I have for my helpers people of short memories."

Never a word more said Kalamake, nor referred again to that affair. But it ran all the while in Keola's head—if he were lazy before, he would now do nothing.

"Why should I work," thought he, "when I have a father-in-law who makes dollars of seashells?"

Presently his share was spent. He spent it all upon fine clothes. And then he was sorry:

"For," thought he, "I had done better to have bought a concertina, with which I might have entertained myself all day long." And then he began to grow vexed with Kalamake.

"This man has the soul of a dog," thought he. "He can gather dollars when he pleases on the beach, and he leaves me to pine for a concertina! Let him beware; I am no child, I am as cunning as he, and hold his secret." With that he spoke to his wife Lehua, and complained of her father's manners.

"I would let my father be," said Lehua. "He is a dangerous man to cross."

"I care that for him!" cried Keola; and snapped his fingers. "I have him by the nose. I can make him do what I please." And he told Lehua the story.

But she shook her head.

"You may do what you like," said she; "but as sure as you thwart my father, you will be no more heard of. Think of this person, and that person; think of Hua, who was a noble of the House of Representatives, and went to Honolulu every year; and not a bone or a hair of him was found. Remember Kamau, and how he wasted to a thread, so that his wife lifted him with one hand. Keola, you are a baby in my father's hands; he will take you with his thumb and finger and eat you like a shrimp."

Now Keola was truly afraid of Kalamake, but he was vain too, and these words of his wife's incensed him.

"Very well," said he, "if that is what you think of me, I will show how much you are deceived." And he went straight to where his father-in-law was sitting in the parlor.

"Kalamake," said he, "I want a concertina."

"Do you, indeed?" said Kalamake.

"Yes," said he, "and I may as well tell you plainly, I mean to have it. A man who picks up dollars on the beach can certainly afford a concertina."

"I had no idea you had so much spirit," replied the sorcerer. "I thought you were a timid, useless lad, and I cannot describe how much pleased I am to find I was mistaken. Now I begin to think I may have found an assistant and successor in my difficult business. A concertina? You shall have the best in Honolulu. And tonight, as soon as it is dark, you and I will go and find the money."

"Shall we return to the beach?" asked Keola.

"No, no!" replied Kalamake; "you must begin to learn more of my secrets. Last time I taught you to pick shells; this time I shall teach you to catch fish. Are you strong enough to launch Pili's boat?"

"I think I am," returned Keola. "But why should we not take your own, which is afloat already?"

"I have a reason which you will understand thoroughly before tomorrow," said Kalamake. "Pili's boat is the better suited for my purpose. So, if you please, let us meet there as soon as it is dark. In the meanwhile, let us keep our own counsel, for there is no cause to let the family into our business."

Honey is not more sweet than was the voice of Kalamake, and Keola could scarce contain his satisfaction.

"I might have had my concertina weeks ago," thought he, "and there is nothing needed in this world but a little courage."

Presently after, he spied Lehua weeping, and was half in a mind to tell her all was well.

"But no," thinks he; "I shall wait till I can show her the concertina; we shall see what the chit will do then. Perhaps she will understand in the future that her husband is a man of some intelligence."

As soon as it was dark father- and son-in-law launched Pili's boat and set the sail. There was a great sea, and it blew strong from the leeward; but the boat was swift and light and dry, and skimmed the waves. The wizard had a lantern, which he lit and held with his finger through the ring; and the two sat in the stern and smoked cigars, and spoke like friends of magic and the great sums of money which they could make by its exercise, and what they should buy first, and what second; and Kalamake talked like a father.

Presently he looked all about, and above him at the stars, and back at the island, which was already three parts sunk under the sea, and he seemed to consider ripely his position.

"Look!" says he, "there is Molokai already far behind us, and Maui like a cloud; and by the bearing of these three stars I know I am come where I desire. This part of the sea is called the Sea of the Dead. It is in this place extraordinarily deep, and the floor is all covered with the bones of men, and in the holes of this part gods and goblins keep their habitation. The flow of the sea is to the north, stronger than a shark can swim, and any man who shall here be thrown out of a ship it bears away like a wild horse into the uttermost ocean. Presently he is spent and goes down, and his bones are scattered with the rest, and gods devour his spirit."

Fear came on Keola at the words, and he looked, and by the light of the stars and the lantern, the warlock seemed to change.

"What ails you?" cried Keola, quick and sharp.

"It is not I who am ailing," said the wizard; "but there is one here very sick."

With that he changed his grasp upon the lantern, and, be-hold! as he drew his finger from the ring, the finger stuck and the ring was burst, and his hand was grown to be of the bigness of three.

At that sight Keola screamed and covered his face.

But Kalamake held up the lantern. "Look rather at my face!" said he—and his head was huge as a barrel; and still he grew and grew as a cloud grows on a mountain, and Keola sat before him screaming, and the boat raced on the great seas.

"And now," said the wizard, "what do you think about that concertina? and are you sure you would not rather have a flute? No?" says he; "that is well, for I do not like my family to be changeable of purpose. But I begin to think I had better get out of this paltry boat, for my bulk swells to a very unusual degree, and if we are not the more careful, she will presently be swamped."

With that he threw his legs over the side. Even as he did so, the greatness of the man grew thirty-fold and forty-fold as swift as sight or thinking, so that he stood in the deep seas to the armpits, and his head and shoulders rose like a high isle, and the swell beat and burst upon his bosom, as it beats and breaks against a cliff. The boat ran still to the north but he reached out his hand, and took the gunwale by the finger and thumb, and broke the side like a biscuit, and Keola was spilled into the sea. And the pieces of the boat the sorcerer crushed in the hollow of his hand and flung miles away into the night.

"Excuse my taking the lantern," said he; "for I have a

long wade before me, and the land is far, and the bottom of the sea uneven, and I feel the bones under my toes."

And he turned and went off walking with great strides; and as often as Keola sank in the trough he could see him no longer; but as often as he was heaved upon the crest, there he was striding and dwindling, and he held the lamp high over his head, and the waves broke white about him as he went.

Since first the islands were fished out of the sea, there was never a man so terrified as this Keola. He swam indeed, but he swam as puppies swim when they are cast in to drown, and knew not wherefore. He could but think of the hugeness of the swelling of the warlock, of that face which was great as a mountain, of those shoulders that were broad as an isle, and of the seas that beat on them in vain. He thought, too, of the concertina, and shame took hold upon him; and of the dead men's bones, and fear shook him.

Of a sudden he was aware of something dark against the stars that tossed, and a light below, and a brightness of the cloven sea; and he heard speech of men. He cried out aloud and a voice answered; and in a twinkling the bows of a ship hung above him on a wave like a thing balanced, and swooped down. He caught with his two hands in the chains of her, and the next moment was buried in the rushing seas, and the next hauled on board by seamen.

They gave him biscuits and dry clothes, and asked him how he came where they found him, and whether the light which they had seen was the lighthouse, Lae o Ka Laau. But Keola knew white men are like children and only believe their own stories; so about himself he told them what he pleased, and as for the light (which was Kalamake's lantern) he vowed he had seen none.

This ship was a schooner bound for Honolulu, and then to trade in the low islands; and by a very good chance for Keola she had lost a man off the bowsprit in a squall. It was no use talking. Keola durst not stay in the Eight Islands. Word goes so quickly, and all men are so fond to talk and carry news, that if he hid in the north end of Kauai or in the south end of Kau, the wizard would have wind of it before a month, and he must perish. So he did what seemed the most prudent, and shipped sailor in the place of the man who had been drowned.

In some ways the ship was a good place. The food was extraordinarily rich and plenty, with biscuits and salt beef every day, and pea-soup and puddings made of flour and suet twice a week, so that Keola grew fat. The captain also was a good man, and the crew no worse than other whites.

The trouble was the mate, who was the most difficult man to please Keola had ever met with, and beat and cursed him daily, both for what he did and what he did not. The blows that he dealt were very sure, for he was strong; and the words he used were very unpalatable, for Keola was come of a good family and accustomed to respect. And what was the worst of all, whenever Keola found a chance to sleep, there was the mate awake and stirring him up with a rope's end. Keola saw it would never do; and he made up his mind to run away.

They were about a month out from Honolulu when they made the land. It was a fine starry night, the sea was smooth as well as the sky fair; and there was the island on their weather bow, a ribbon of palm trees lying flat along the sea. The captain and the mate looked at it with the night glass, and named the name of it, and talked of it, beside the wheel where Keola was steering. It seemed it was an isle where no traders came. By the captain's way, it was an isle besides where no man dwelt; but the mate thought otherwise.

"I don't give a cent for the directory," said he. "I've been past here one night in the schooner *Eugénie*. It was just such a night as this. They were fishing with torches, and the beach was thick with lights like a town."

"Well, well," says the captain, "it's steep-to, that's the great point; and there ain't any outlying dangers by the chart, so we'll just hug the lee side of it. Keep her ramping full, don't I tell you!" he cried to Keola, who was listening so hard that he forgot to steer.

And the mate cursed him, and swore that if he got started after him with a belaying pin, it would be a cold day for Keola.

And then the captain and mate went away, and Keola was left to himself.

"This island will do very well for me," he thought; "if no traders deal there, the mate will never come. And as for Kalamake, it is not possible he can ever get as far as this."

With that he kept edging the schooner nearer in. He had to do this quietly, for the trouble with these white men, and above all with the mate, was that you could never be sure of them. They would all be sleeping sound, or else pretending, and if a sail shook, they would jump to their feet and fall on you with a rope's end. So Keola edged her up little by little. And presently the land was close on board, and the sound of the sea on the sides of it grew loud.

With that, the mate sat up suddenly.

"What are you doing?" he roars. "You'll have the ship ashore!"

And he made one bound for Keola, and Keola made another clean over the rail and plump into the starry sea. When he came up again, the schooner had payed off on her true course, and the mate stood by the wheel himself, and Keola heard him cursing. The sea was smooth under the lee of the island; it was warm besides, and Keola had his sailor's knife, so he had no fear of sharks. A little way before him the trees stopped; there was a break in the line of the land like the mouth of a harbor; and the tide, which was then flowing, took him up and carried him through. One minute he was without, and the next within, and floated there in a wide shallow water, and all about him was the ring of the land, with its string of palm trees. And he was amazed, because this was a kind of island he had never heard of.

The time of Keola in that place was in two periods—the period when he was alone, and the period when he was there with the tribe. At first he sought everywhere and found no man; only some houses standing in a hamlet, and the marks of fires. But the ashes of the fires were cold and the rains had washed them away; and the winds had blown, and some of the huts were overthrown. It was here he took his dwelling. He made a fire drill, and a shell hook, and fished and cooked his fish, and climbed after green cocoanuts, the juice of which he drank, for in all the isle there was no water. The days were long to him, and the nights terrifying. He made a lamp of cocoa shell, and drew the oil of the ripe nuts, and made a wick of fiber; and when evening came he closed up his hut, and lit his lamp and lay and trembled till morning. Many a time he thought in his heart he would have been better in the bottom of the sea, his bones rolling there with the others.

All this while he kept by the inside of the island, for the huts were on the shore of the lagoon, and it was there the palms grew best, and the lagoon itself abounded with good fish. And to the other side he went once only, and he looked but once at the beach of the ocean, and came away shaking. For the look of it, with its bright sand, and strewn shells, and strong sun and surf went sore against his inclination.

"It cannot be," he thought, "and yet it is very like. And how do I know? These white men, although they pretend to know where they are sailing, must take their chance like other people. So that after all we may have sailed in a circle, and I may be quite near to Molokai, and this may be the very beach where my father-in-law gathered his dollars."

So after that he was prudent, and kept to the land-side.

It was perhaps a month later, when the people of the place

arrived—the fill of six great boats. They were a fine race of men, and spoke a tongue that sounded very different from the tongue of Hawaii, but so many of the words were the same that it was not difficult to understand. The men were very courteous, and the women very kind. They made Keola welcome, and built him a house, and gave him a wife; and what surprised him the most, he was never sent to work with the young men.

And now Keola had three periods. First he had a period of being very sad, and then he had a period when he was pretty merry. Last of all came the third, when he was the most terrified man in the four oceans.

The cause of the first period was the girl he had to wife. He was in doubt about the island, and he might have been in doubt about the speech, of which he had heard so little when he came there with the wizard on the mat. But about his wife there was no mistake conceivable, for she was the same girl who ran from him crying in the wood. So he had sailed all this way, and might as well have stayed in Molokai; and had left home and wife and all his friends for no other cause but to escape his enemy. And the place he had come to was the wizard's hunting ground, and the place where he walked invisible. It was at this period when he kept most close to the lagoon-side, and as far as he dared, abode in the cover of his hut.

The cause of the second period was talk he heard from his wife and the chief islanders. Keola himself said little. He was never so sure of his new friends, for he judged they were too civil to be wholesome, and since he had grown better acquainted with his father-in-law the man had grown more cautious. So he told them nothing of himself, but only his name and descent, and that he came from the Eight Islands, and about the King's paiace in Honolulu, and how he was a chief friend of the King and the missionaries. But he put many questions and learned much.

The island where he was was called the Isle of Voices. It

belonged to the tribe, but they made their home upon another, three hours' sail to the southward. There they lived and had their permanent houses, and it was a rich island, where there were eggs and chickens and pigs, and ships came trading with rum and tobacco. It was there the schooner had gone after Keola deserted; there, too, the mate had died. It seems, when the ship came, it was the beginning of the sickly season in that isle, when the fish of the lagoon are poisonous, and all who eat of them swell up and die. The mate was told of it. He saw the boats preparing, because in that season the people leave that island and sail to the Isle of Voices; but he was a fool of a white man, who would believe no stories but his own, and he caught one of these fish, cooked it and ate it, and swelled up and died.

As for the Isle of Voices, it lay solitary the most part of the year. Only now and then a boat's crew came for copra, and in the bad season, when the fish at the main isle were poisonous, the tribe dwelt there in a body. It had its name from a marvel, for it seemed the sea-side of it was all beset with invisible devils; day and night you heard them talking with one another in strange tongues. Day and night little fires blazed up and were extinguished on the beach; and what was the cause of these doings no man might conceive. Keola asked them if it were the same in their own island where they stayed, and they told him no, not there; nor yet in any other of some hundred isles that lay all about them in that sea. It was a thing peculiar to the Isle of Voices. They told him also that these fires and voices were ever on the sea-side and in the seaward fringes of the wood, and a man might dwell by the lagoon two thousand years (if he could live so long) and never be any way troubled; and even on the sea-side the devils did no harm if let alone. Only once a chief had cast a spear at one of the voices, and the same night he fell out of a cocoanut palm and was killed.

Keola thought a good bit with himself. He saw he would be all right when the tribe returned to the main island, and right enough where he was, if he kept by the lagoon, yet he had a mind to make things righter if he could. So he told the high chief he had once been in an isle that was pestered the same way, and the folk had found a means to cure that trouble.

"There was a tree growing in the bush there," says he, "and it seems these devils came to get the leaves of it. So the people of the isle cut down the tree wherever it was found, and the devils came no more."

They asked what kind of a tree this was, and he showed them the tree of which Kalamake burned the leaves. They found it hard to believe, yet the idea tickled them. Night after night the old men debated it in their councils, but the high chief (though he was a brave man) was afraid of the matter, and reminded them daily of the chief who cast a spear against the voices and was killed. The thought of that brought everything to a standstill again.

Though he could not yet bring about the destruction of the trees, Keola was well enough pleased, and began to look about him and take pleasure in his days. Among other things, he was kinder to his wife, so that the girl began to love him greatly. One day he came to the hut, and she lay on the ground lamenting.

"Why," said Keola, "what is wrong with you now?"

She declared it was nothing.

The same night she woke him. The lamp burned very low, but he saw by her face she was in sorrow.

"Keola," she said, "put your ear to my mouth that I may whisper, for no one must hear us. Two days before the boats begin to be got ready, go to the sea-side of the isle and lie in a thicket. We shall choose that place beforehand, you and I, and hide food. And every night I shall come near by there singing. So when a night comes and you do not hear me, you shall know we are clean gone out of the island, and you may come forth again in safety."

The soul of Keola died within him.

"What is this?" he cried. "I cannot live among devils. I will not be left behind upon this isle. I am dying to leave it."

"You will never leave it alive, my dear Keola," said the girl; "for to tell you the truth, my people are eaters of men; but this they keep secret. And the reason they will kill you before we leave is because in our island ships come, and there is a white trader there in a house with a veranda. Oh, that is a fine place indeed! The trader has barrels filled with flour, and a French warship once came in the lagoon and gave everybody wine and biscuit. Ah, my poor Keola, I wish I could take you there, for great is my love for you, and it is the finest place in the seas except Papeete."

So now Keola was the most terrified man in the four oceans. He had heard tell of eaters of men in the south islands, and the thing had always been a fear to him; and here it was knocking at his door. He had heard besides, from travelers, of their practices, and how when they are in a mind to eat a man, they cherish and fondle him like a mother with a favorite baby. And he saw this must be his own case; and that was why he had been housed, and fed, and liberated from all work; and why the old men and the chiefs discoursed with him like a person of weight. So he lay on his bed and railed upon his destiny; and the flesh curdled on his bones.

The next day the people of the tribe were very civil, as their way was. They were elegant speakers, and they made beautiful poetry, and jested at meals. It was little enough Keola cared for their fine ways. All he saw was the white teeth shining in their mouths, and his gorge rose at the sight. And when they were done eating, he went and lay in the bush like a dead man.

The next day it was the same, and then his wife followed him.

"Keola," she said, "if you do not eat, I tell you plainly you will be killed and cooked tomorrow. Some of the old chiefs are murmuring already. They think you are fallen sick and must lose flesh."

With that Keola got to his feet, and anger burned in him.

"It is little I care one way or the other," said he. "I am between the devil and the deep sea. Since die I must, let me die the quickest way. And since I must be eaten at the best of it, let me rather be eaten by hobgoblins than by men. Farewell," said he, and he left her standing, and walked to the sea-side of the island.

It was all bare in the strong sun. There was no sign of man, only the beach was trodden, and all about him as he went, the voices talked and whispered, and the little fires sprang up and burned down. All tongues of the earth were spoken there: the French, the Dutch, the Russian, the Tamil, the Chinese. Whatever land knew sorcery, there were some of its people whispering in Keola's ear. And as he walked he saw the shells vanish before him, and no man to pick them up. I think the devil would have been afraid to be alone in such a company; but Keola was past fear and courted death. When the fires sprang up, he charged for them like a bull. Bodiless voices called to and fro; unseen hands poured sand upon the flames; and they were gone from the beach before he reached them.

"It is plain Kalamake is not here," he thought, "or I would have been killed long since."

With that he sat him down in the margin of the wood, for he was tired, and put his chin upon his hands. The business before his eyes continued; the beach babbled with voices, and the fires sprang up and sank, and the shells vanished and were renewed again even while he looked.

"It was a by-day when I was here before," he thought, "for it was nothing to this."

And his head was dizzy with the thought of these millions

and millions of dollars, and all these hundreds and hundreds of persons culling them upon the beach and flying in the air higher and swifter than eagles.

"And to think how they have fooled me with their talk of mints," says he, "when it is clear that all the new coin in all the world is gathered on these sands! But I will know better the next time!" said he.

And at last, he knew not very well how or when, sleep fell on Keola, and he forgot the island and all his sorrows.

Early the next day, before the sun was up, a bustle woke him. He awoke in fear, for he thought the tribe had caught him napping; but it was no such matter. Only, on the beach in front of him, the bodiless voices called and shouted, and it seemed they all passed and swept beside him up the coast of the island.

"What is afoot now?" thinks Keola. And it was plain to him it was something beyond ordinary, for the fires were not lighted nor the shells taken, but the bodiless voices kept posting up the beach, and hailing and dying away; and by the sound of them these wizards were angry.

"It is not me they are angry at," thought Keola, "for they pass me close."

As when hounds go by, or horses in a race, or city folk coursing to a fire, and all men join and follow after, so it was now with Keola; and he knew not what he did, nor why he did it, but there, lo and behold! he was running with the voices.

So he turned one point of the island, and this brought him in view of a second; and there he remembered the wizard trees to have been growing by the score together in a wood. From this point there went up a hubbub of men crying; and by the sound of them, those that he ran with shaped their course for the same quarter. A little nearer, and there began to mingle with the outcry the crash of many axes. And at this the thought came into his mind that the high chief had

at last consented; that the men of the tribe had set to cutting down these trees; that word had gone about the isle
from sorcerer to sorcerer, and these were all now assembling
to defend their trees. Desire of strange things swept him on.
He posted with the voices, crossed the beach, and came into
the borders of the wood, and stood astonished. One tree had
fallen, others were part hewed away. There was the tribe
clustered. They were back to back, and bodies lay, and blood
flowed among their feet. The hue of fear was on all their
faces; their voices went up to heaven shrill as a weasel's cry.

Have you seen a child when he is all alone and has a
wooden sword, and fights, leaping and hewing with the empty
air? Even so the man-eaters huddled back to back and heaved
up their axes, and laid on, and screamed as they laid on, and
behold! no man to contend with them! only here and there
Keola saw an axe swinging over against them without hands;
and time and again a man of the tribe would fall before it,
clove in twain or burst asunder, and his soul sped howling.

For a while Keola looked upon this like one who dreams,
and then fear took him by the midst as sharp as death, that
he should behold such doings. Even in that same flash the
high chief of the clan espied him standing, and pointed and
called out his name. Thereat the whole tribe saw him also,
and their eyes flashed, and their teeth clashed.

"I am here too long," thought Keola, and ran farther out
of the wood and down the beach, not caring whither.

"Keola!" said a voice close by upon the empty sand.

"Lehua! is that you?" he cried, and gasped, and looked in
vain for her.

"I saw you pass before," the voice answered; "but you
would not hear me. Quick! get the leaves and herbs, and let
us flee."

"You are there with the mat?" he asked.

"Here, at your side," said she. And he felt her arms about
him. "Quick! the leaves and the herbs, before my father can
get back!"

So Keola ran for his life, and fetched the wizard fuel; and Lehua guided him back, and set his feet upon the mat, and made the fire. All the time of its burning, the sound of the battle towered out of the wood; the wizards and the man-eaters hard at fight; the wizards, the viewless ones, roaring out aloud like bulls upon the mountain, and the men of the tribe replying shrill and savage out of the terror of their souls. And all the time of the burning, Keola stood there and listened, and shook, and watched how the unseen hands of Lehua poured the leaves. She poured them fast, and the flame burned high, and scorched Keola's hands; and she speeded and blew the burning with her breath. The last leaf was eaten, the flame fell, and the shock followed, and there were Keola and Lehua in the room at home.

Now, when Keola could see his wife at last he was mighty pleased, and he was mighty pleased to be home again in Molokai and sit down beside a bowl of poi—for they make no poi on board ships, and there was none in the Isle of Voices—and to be clean escaped out of the hands of the eaters of men. But there was another matter not so clear, and Lehua and Keola talked of it all night and were troubled. There was Kalamake left upon the isle. If, by the blessing of God, he could but stick there, all were well; but should he escape and return to Molokai, it would be an ill day for his daughter and her husband. They spoke of his gift of swelling, and whether he could wade that distance in the seas. But Keola knew by this time where that island was—and that is to say, in the Low or Dangerous Archipelago. So they fetched the atlas and looked upon the distance in the map, and by what they could make of it, it seemed a far way for an old gentleman to walk. Still, it would not do to make too sure of a warlock like Kalamake, and they determined at last to take counsel of a white missionary.

So the first one that came by Keola told him everything. And the missionary was very sharp on him for taking the second wife in the low island; but for all the rest, he vowed he could make neither head nor tail of it.

"However," says he, "if you think this money of your father's ill-gotten, my advice to you would be give some of it to the lepers and some to the missionary fund. And as for this extraordinary rigmarole, you cannot do better than keep it to yourselves."

But he warned the police at Honolulu that, by all he could make out, Kalamake and Keola had been coining false money, and it would not be amiss to watch them.

Keola and Lehua took his advice, and gave many dollars to the lepers and the fund. And no doubt the advice must have been good, for from that day to this, Kalamake has never more been heard of. But whether he was slain in the battle by the trees, or whether he is still kicking his heels upon the Isle of Voices, who shall say?